JOE HALDEMAN, born in 1943, graduated in physics and astronomy and did postgraduate work in mathematics and computer science. He was drafted and sent as a combat engineer to Vietnam, where he was wounded. After WAR YEAR and two other novels, came his success in the Science Fiction field with the publication of THE FOREVER WAR, which won a Nebula award and his first Hugo award.

Other Avon Books by
Joe Haldeman

ALL MY SINS REMEMBERED
INFINITE DREAMS
MINDBRIDGE
STUDY WAR NO MORE

WAR YEAR

JOE HALDEMAN

AVON
PUBLISHERS OF BARD, CAMELOT, DISCUS AND FLARE BOOKS

AVON BOOKS
A division of
The Hearst Corporation
1790 Broadway
New York, New York 10019

First Avon Printing, December, 1984

AVON TRADEMARK REG. U. S. PAT. OFF. AND IN
OTHER COUNTRIES, MARCA REGISTRADA, HECHO EN
U. S. A.

Printed in the U. S. A.

WFH 10 9 8 7 6 5 4 3 2 1

FOR THE MEMORY OF
FARMER AND DOC AND SERGEANT CROWDER.

CHAPTER ONE

I almost slept through that first enemy attack.

I'd been on KP all day, washing dishes, on my feet from dawn to dark. When it was over, I went to my bunk and just slept like a rock. So I didn't hear the sirens when they went off. I woke up with this big guy shaking me.

"Incoming, man, wake up! Goddammit, incoming!" And he made for the door.

I didn't know what "incoming" meant, but he looked pretty shook. Then I woke up enough to hear that the sirens were blasting the way they warned us would happen in case of an attack on Cam Ranh Bay. I jumped out of bed and nearly caught that guy at the bottom of the steps.

I could hear something going *crump—crump* off in the distance. I didn't know how far off they were, but at least I couldn't see any explosions. Followed the big guy to the nearest bunker—that's just a big sewer pipe sitting on the ground, covered with sandbags—and crawled in after him.

It was right crowded, and the pipe wasn't big enough for a tall Oklahoman, like yours truly, to sit without cracking his head on the top.

"You fellas are a little late for the party. Decide to catch a few more minutes shut-eye?"

"Man, I was on KP all day," I said. "Never even heard the sirens until this guy woke me up."

"Maybe he should've let you sleep. Those're 122's

comin' down—one of 'em hits this bunker and we'll all be blown away anyhow."

"Tell'em all about it, hard-core," somebody else said.

I got this weird feeling in my stomach. I guess everybody who goes to Vietnam knows there's some chance he'll get killed. But the first week? For Christ's sake!

There was a high, thin whistle. You could hardly hear it over the sirens. Then a loud *crump!*

"Gettin' a little closer. Like I say, those're 122-milli-meter rockets from China; they'll go through ten layers of sandbags just like they weren't there. This bunker's got four, maybe five layers. So if one hits us, we won't even know what happened."

I was so scared I wanted to puke. Wanted to run, too, but I knew there wasn't any place safer than here.

There was another loud one, and then they stopped. The sirens stopped, too, after a while. In about half an hour, a guy stuck his head in the bunker and said, "All clear, boys." We got out of the bunker and went back to our bunks. But I was still too nervous to sleep.

I was still awake, just staring at the ceiling, when they called the first formation of the day. It was about ten o'clock.

There were a couple of hundred of us lined up on what they called the "hot sheet." Sheets of steel soaking up the Vietnam sun and pushing it back through the soles of your boots. You stand at attention while a sergeant yells at you through a bullhorn.

"Following named personnel," he yelled, "line up over in the shade. You're goin' to Play-koo tomorrow morning, 14 January, uh, 1968."

Pleiku, I thought. It's been in the papers.

"Adams, Donald, RA 67948563. Barnes, Abraham, US 23746894. Brown, Leon . . ."

I stood and waited for the F's to come up. We'd done this for over an hour every day for nearly a week, and my name hadn't been called yet.

". . . Farmer, John, US 11575278."

That's me. I broke out of the formation and carried my

gear to the bunch standing in the shade. Off the hot sheet it must have been thirty degrees cooler. A buck-sergeant—three stripes, nothing to be afraid of—was in charge of us. When they finished the alphabet, he led us away. We went into a big white-painted shack, same kind as I'd stayed in the past week.

"This is your billet for the night, men. Tomorrow morning at 0400 you'll be leaving for Pleiku. You've been here long enough to know the rules—if you hear the siren, hightail it into the bunker next door. If you hear shots and no siren, take the mattress off the bed and roll up in it and pray. No John Wayne stuff, right? You'll get your chance, where you're headed."

He really knew how to make a fella feel good.

I didn't feel like waiting in the chow line, so I went over and waited for the club to open. The club was just another white shack, but you could get hamburgers and beer there. I was getting used to beer—in Oklahoma a nineteen-year-old can't get it, but here, nobody asks how old you are.

There were about a dozen of us waiting when they opened the door. I got a hamburger and a warm beer and sat down at a table. Took out a tablet and started to write a letter to my girl, Wendy.

"Mind if we sit down here?" Two guys; dark tan and shaggy moustaches showed they must've been in Vietnam a while.

"Suit yourself." I went back to writing my letter.

"You a new guy?" one of them asked after a minute.

"Yeah, I've only been here a week."

"Where you headed—got your orders yet?"

I took the orders out of my pocket, unfolded them, and laid them on the table. "Pleiku—Fourth Administration Battalion."

They both laughed. "You poor fucker—you might wind up in our outfit!" the taller one said. "Fourth Engineers—I'm Smitty and this runt's Shakey; we're both in Company C."

"What makes your outfit so bad?"

"Oh, there's nothin' wrong with it—if you don't mind gettin' shot at."

"Come on, Smitty, it's not that rough."

"Sure, it isn't—you tell him how you got the name Shakey!"

"So I get nervous sometimes . . ."

"Nervous is the only way to *be*—" I noticed something a little stronger than beer on Smitty's breath—"be first in the hole and last out. Behind a tree if there's no hole, diggin' a hole if there's no tree . . ."

"Cut it out, Smitty, you're plastered. You're gonna scare the poor guy to death. It's not all that bad, buddy."

"Name's John Farmer."

"Way you talk, they'll call you Tex."

"I'm from Oklahoma . . ."

"Man, this is the army—they'll *still* call you Tex."

Smitty got up from the table and walked away, not too steady. "Back in a minute," he mumbled.

Shakey watched him wander out the door and shook his head. "He's gonna go pass out. He'll wake up sick in the morning and be hittin' that bottle again before noon."

"He do this all the time?"

"Nah—for one thing, there's no liquor out in the boonies. Even if there was, Smitty wouldn't get drunk. Not too many people would. Everybody depends on everybody else.

"But Smitty's on vacation—he's headed for Bangkok for R & R."

"R and R?"

"Yeah, rest and recreation—didn't they tell you about that? After you've been in Vietnam long enough, you get a week's vacation. Bangkok, Hawaii, Australia—there's a couple of dozen places you can go. Can't go back to the world, though. Guess they're afraid you'll stay."

We sat for a minute without saying anything. "Shakey, if you don't mind me asking—why *do* they call you that?"

"Good reason. The first fuckin' day I was out with the company, they ran into an ambush, lost thirty men. I didn't see how anybody could live through a *week* of that, let alone a year. Things are pretty cool most of the time,

Joe Haldeman

everybody told me, but I couldn't make myself believe it. I was pretty shook for a month or two."

He took out a pipe and started loading it with tobacco. "I learned, though. Doesn't pay to sweat it. You'll either make it or you won't. Most people do make it."

He lit the pipe. The warm sweet smoke reminded me of my father. "I've been kind of hoping they'd make me a clerk," I said. "I took typing in high school; passed the army typing test."

"Wouldn't bet on it. What's your MOS?"

Yeah, that was the bad part. My MOS, Military Occupational Specialty. "Combat Engineer."

"Hmmm . . . you might wind up in our outfit, at that. But I don't think they'll make you a clerk. Hell, we've got a college graduate out there humpin' the boonies with us."

"Humpin' the boonies?"

"Man, don't you know anything? Humpin' the boonies— that's what you'll probably be doing the next twelve months. You put a monster pack on your back, a gun in one hand and a shovel in the other, and you go out in the woods—the boondocks, man, the boonies—lookin' for trouble. Find it, too, sooner or later."

"Really bad, then?" and he was talking about Smitty scaring me.

"Oh, I dunno." He smiled. "I got through a whole year of it without a single scratch."

"What, you're headed home?"

"That's right, man, I'm a real short-timer. *Really* short. Two more days and I get on that bird and kiss this hole goodbye. You might even be my replacement."

"That'd be funny."

"No, happens all the time. You figure everybody goin' to Pleiku spends a week here at Cam Ranh Bay first, and everybody leavin' has to hang around here for a week . . . a guy's replacement almost has to be here when he's checkin' out. Just a question of running into him."

"You ever meet the guy you replaced?"

"Nah." Shakey drank the rest of his beer in one gulp

11

and set the empty can down carefully. "He went home in a box."

"Sorry; I . . ."

"Don't be—get sorry over strangers dying and you'll spend the rest of your life being sorry." He relit his pipe and stood up. "Well, better go check on Smitty. Take it easy, Tex. Hope you have half the luck I did."

"Have a good trip home." Kind of a dumb thing to say.

"No such thing as a bad trip home." He gave me a peace sign and walked out the door.

Going home in a box, I had to think, would be a bad trip home.

I stuck a beer under my shirt—you aren't supposed to take them out of the club—and walked out into the cool night. I swear the temperature here must drop fifty degrees when the sun goes down. You can wake up cold and be frying by nine.

They were fighting a few miles south of Cam Ranh Bay. Something was going on there every night since I landed. They told us not to worry about it. Guess I was in a worrying mood, though.

I sat down on the sand behind our billet and watched the fireworks on the horizon. There were a couple of planes, propeller jobs, and a helicopter shooting up the landscape with machine guns and rockets. Looked impressive, red and orange flames, but you couldn't hear anything. I guess it'd even look pretty if you didn't know what was going on. I watched for maybe half an hour, until I finished the beer, then went back to my billet and sacked out.

Only got a couple of hours' sleep. The buck-sergeant came stomping in, turned on all the lights, and started hollering the most godawful language I'd ever heard—and I've heard some fine stuff. Then he started tipping over bunks when people didn't get up. I squirmed out just in time to keep from getting dumped. The buck-sergeant wasn't happy at being up at three in the morning, and he wanted everybody to know it.

He calmed down a little bit after everybody was up and getting their gear ready. "All right, you fuckers, there's a bus outside the door. Hand me one copy of your orders before you get on. The last ten fuckers gotta stand all the way to the airport, so get a move on."

I was the second one on the bus, but it turned out nobody had to stand. Never trust a sergeant. It was only a ten-minute ride, anyhow.

The airport was a big metal hut filled with bored soldiers, and not much else. It had a refreshment stand and a Stars and Stripes book store, but they wouldn't open until 0900. I sat on my duffel bag and started writing letters.

Wrote a long one to my girl and one to Mom. I was halfway through writing my brother when the buck-sergeant made us line up to go out to the plane. He took a roll call, opened the door, and we trotted onto the field. There was a big C-130, a "flying boxcar," and we got on in no particular order. No seats—we just flopped our bags on the metal floor and sat on them. We couldn't get everybody on at first, but they juggled us around and packed us in tight as sardines, and managed to fit everyone in.

An Air Force guy with captain's bars and a tough-looking .45 in a shoulder holster poked his head in from the front of the plane. "I'm your pilot, Captain Platt. I hope none of you guys get airsick too easy—this is gonna be a rough ride.

"This airplane is older than some of you. It'll probably outlive some of you, too. If you got anything to say to your neighbor, you better say it now. 'Cause once I start these engines, you won't be able to even hear yourself think until you get to Pleiku. It's about one hour's flight. If we land any sooner than that, you better start praying. You can smoke as soon as the light goes on." Then he yelled something out a window and the engines started. The noise was incredible, so loud it made my teeth hurt.

I'd flown lots of times before; my Dad had a license. We'd go out on weekends, out by Turner Field, and rent a plane for a few hours. But we'd always get the little Pipers or

13

Cessnas, nothing that made a tenth as much noise as this did.

We stood still for about five minutes before the plane started to move.

After we rolled down the runway a while, the noise doubled and we were in the air. Without windows you could only tell by the upward tilt of the plane and the fact that the air was less bumpy than the ground. Still, the airplane sounded like it was going to shake itself apart.

After a boring hour—nothing to do but look at the other guys turning green—the plane started to come down. I could feel the pressure in my ears, and there was a loud bump when the landing gear came down. We bounced several times before the plane started rolling on the ground.

The rear door fell open before the plane stopped taxiing. You couldn't see much, except that everything was covered with red clay. All over everything was a thick white fog, bright in the morning sunlight.

We rolled to a stop and the unloading ramp clanked down. Everybody scrambled out of that plane as fast as they could.

Sure enough, there was another buck-sergeant there on the runway. He herded us into a line and marched us over to a bus. As we got on the bus, he checked our names off a list.

The bus had metal screens, like thick chicken wire, over the windows. One of the windows had a bullet hole in it. The bus had a name painted over the fender. It was called "Last Chance."

Two guards, armed with machine guns, got on the bus. One of them spoke up: "All right, listen up! If there's any shootin', just get down under the seat and make like a turtle. We'll take care of everything—right, Killer?" The other guy laughed in a dumb kind of way. "We're goin' through Pleiku City. There's lots of VC there who'd just love to knock off a bus fulla green troops. No sweat, though. We ain't lost a bus all week."

Guess we were supposed to be impressed. But I'd been in

the army too long—less than a year at that—and seen too many phony tough guys.

Have to admit I was getting a little scared when we went through the town of Pleiku. It took a long time to get through, too; seemed as big as Tulsa. Half the buidings were demolished. Bullet holes and shell craters everywhere. But there wasn't any fighting going on, just lots of skinny little Orientals who stared at the bus as we went by. None of them smiled.

There were fewer and fewer buildings and after a while we were out in the country. Nothing but red dust and a few scraggly-looking bushes on both sides of the road—looked like the worst part of Oklahoma in the middle of the summer. And this was January.

After a while we got to Camp Enari. A sign said "Welcome to the Fourth Division," but I didn't feel too welcome. It seemed more of a prison camp than an army camp—barbed wire everywhere, sentries with machine guns in towers all around the edge of the camp. A couple of privates rolled aside a big barbed-wire gate, and we drove through.

CHAPTER TWO

"I'd like to welcome all of you to Camp Enari." The major was pacing up and down, looking at the floor. We were lined up all around the walls of the big plywood building. A private was passing out clipboards and a thick wad of forms to each person.

". . . and I'd like to be able to say that you're going to enjoy your stay here. Unfortunately, you *won't* enjoy it— nobody ever has. And you might as well start getting used to the fact that there's a war going on, on the other side of that barbed wire. Nobody's ever gotten killed inside Camp Enari, though we've been attacked a few times. But most of you aren't staying in Enari.

"I'll give you the facts right now. You're going to spend a year—most of you—someplace here in the Central Highlands of Vietnam. Some of you are going home early. About one man in twenty goes home dead. There are about forty men in this building, so figure it out. Maybe the guy standing next to you, maybe the guys on both sides of you . . . maybe you.

"Now I'm not saying this just to scare you—but if you're scared, you're smart. You've got a much better chance to get home in one piece if you're scared—careful scared, healthy scared—every day of the next three hundred and fifty-some. The guy who gets cocky, the careless one, he's the one who doesn't watch where he puts his foot and steps on a mine. He's the one who lights up a cigarette at night and gets a sniper's bullet through his brain. Or doesn't keep his weapon clean and has it jam up when it could save his life.

"That's your first warning. You'll get lots more in the next week. There'll be training every day from 0600 in the morning—pay attention to every word these men tell you. They're all combat veterans, and they'll be trying to teach you how to stay alive for a year.

"Now I'm going to turn you over to Sergeant Ford, who'll help you fill out the forms. Good luck."

A short blond sergeant, with a face like a monkey, who had been sitting on the floor, walked to the center of the room. "Okay, troops, listen up!" A sergeant knows nobody ever listens to him, so he has to say "listen up" before he says anything important.

"The pink slip of paper on top there is what they call a release. The army's going to send a telegram to your old lady if you get killed or hurt really bad. If you can read, you'll see that this pink form asks whether you want a telegram sent if you're 'lightly wounded.' Just check 'yes' or 'no' and sign it. If you're smart, you'll check 'no.' You don't want your old lady to freak out just because you got a little hole in your head. Right?"

That made sense, even if I didn't care for the way he said it. I checked "no" and signed it.

It went on like that for a couple of hours, while we filled out the rest of the forms. Some of them could scare you if you stopped to think about what they meant, like that first one, and the one that took care of where to send your body . . . but most of them were just regular army stuff, about your pay and where you were born and how old your mother is and all that stuff. I must have written my address a hundred times. When we finally got up to leave, my hand was ready to fall off from writing so much.

We left that place and walked through the scorching sun to Supply, another big shack like all the others. We just walked through in a line and they piled stuff in our arms—some clothes, first-aid packet, a canteen and mess gear so we could eat and drink, a steel helmet—steel "pot," they call it—to keep our brains inside in case there was an attack, and for sleeping, a couple of sheets, a mosquito net, and a blanket—must be 130 degrees out there, and they give us a blanket! We each got two boxes of malaria pills and a little bottle of pills for purifying water.

Then they led us to our billet and showed us how to tie the mosquito nets over our bunks, to keep from being eaten alive during the night. I hadn't noticed any mosquitoes around, but they said they really get thick after sundown.

By the time I got my bed made and the net strung up, almost everybody else had left for lunch. I took my mess kit—just a metal bowl with knife, fork and spoon attached—and went out to find the chow hall.

Turns out I walked right by it, on the wrong side. I waded through the thick dust for a couple of blocks—the dust was fine as talcum powder, dark red, and piled up in drifts above your ankles. Finally I stopped a guy and asked directions. He sent me back to the mess hall, and this time I passed the right side. There was a long line, not moving, and I went to the end of it.

Just then a siren started to blow. I nearly jumped out of my skin and started looking for a bunker to run to.

The guy in front of me turned around and smiled. "Man, don't sweat it . . . that's just the noontime whistle. Don't mean anything unless it blows some other time—then you wanta jump."

"Thanks—guess I'm a little jumpy." I stuck out my hand. "Name's John Farmer."

"Wally Lewis." He was short and stocky. "Guess you're new around this place—been assigned yet?"

"No, just got here today. They say we've got to go to a bunch of classes before we get assigned."

"Right . . . you get to play soldier for a few days. Just hope you don't have to *be* one, though. A lot of guys get assigned here in base camp. Never have to shoot a gun again, after that first week."

"That'd suit me fine. I never asked to be part of this war."

18

Wally laughed. "Man, who ever did?"

We talked for about twenty minutes, while the line moved up. Wally was a clerk for one of the infantry companies. Wasn't always a clerk, though—he started out as a rifleman. After six weeks in the boonies he got shot in the arm. He showed me the scar, bright pink against his brown skin. When he got out of the hospital, the clerk job was open and he grabbed it. He'd been behind a desk ever since.

Like the major, Wally said nobody had ever gotten killed inside the base camp, Camp Enari. But it still paid to be careful. People had been hurt in three rocket and mortar attacks, and it was just luck that nobody had died.

There was a rumor, Wally said, that Enari would get another attack around midnight. But that rumor came around at least twice a week. He said it wasn't worth worrying about.

Wally was only in this part of camp—fourth Admin—to round up some new men who had been assigned to his outfit. After chow he went off to find them and I went back to my billet.

Some guys were sitting in little groups talking, and a bunch of old sergeants were sitting in the back playing cards and passing around a bottle of whiskey. I flopped down on my bunk and tried to get some sleep. It was too noisy and too hot.

After a while a sergeant came in and rounded us up. We walked out to a black metal shed in back of our billet.

"This here is called a tock," the sergeant said. "There's enough M-16's in here to give you each one and have some left over. Now who's the highest ranking man here?"

One of the sergeants who'd been drinking whiskey, almost bald with a little fringe of white hair, stepped up. "That'd be me, I guess. Master Sergeant Jack O'Donnell."

He opened the tock and gave the key to O'Donnell. "Sarge, you're in charge of givin' these weapons out. Two different times you give 'em out."

He walked inside the dark tock and came out with a clipboard. "When you give 'em out for training, have some-

19

body write down everybody's name and the serial number on the weapon he gets. Use this clipboard and have him put it back in the tock when he's through.

"If there's an attack, just open it up and pass out the guns as fast as you can. I'll come by with ammunition if Charlie gets inside the camp.

"If you leave the area at night, to go to the NCO club or somethin', give the key to someone who'll stay around 'til you get back. Charlie doesn't usually attack before midnight—try to be back by then.

"Now this goes for everybody. Any time you go out after dark, take your steel pot, canteen, and first-aid packet. If there's an attack, get in the nearest trench or bunker. Try to get back here. This is the only place you're goin' to get a gun. Be back here by midnight ev'ry night.

"That's about all for today. You can do whatever you want as long as you're back by midnight. The PX closes in an hour and a half. You probably won't get there for another couple of days, so better go now if you need cigarettes or shavin' stuff. The clubs open at six—that's 1800 for you hard-core types. There'll be a movie outside here soon as it gets dark. Dismissed."

I really wanted something to drink after breathing that dust all day. Since we had a couple of hours before the Enlisted Men's club opened, I followed a bunch of guys down to the PX. I thought maybe I could get a Coke there.

The PX was huge, the size of a big supermarket, and it had just about everything. Everything but Cokes, that is. I picked up some comic books and a little can of pineapple juice. The little Oriental checkout girl opened the can for me.

The juice was good but it just made me thirstier. I went back to the Admin company area and emptied my canteen down my throat. Then I went up to the mess hall to beat the line for dinner. I should have known better.

I was sitting in the shade in front of the mess hall with two other guys, reading about the Fantastic Four. The mess sergeant grabbed the three of us and put us on "serving detail." So I got to eat early, but spent the next hour spooning out mashed potatoes to guys who were smart enough to come late.

After he finally let us go, I was dead tired. I stumbled back to the billet and flopped in my bunk. It had been a rough day, but it was still so hot and noisy that I just couldn't sleep.

A bunch of guys came in wearing just towels and boots. They were actually clean. I looked at myself—red dirt ground into every bit of skin—and asked one of them who told me where the shower was. So I stripped down—looked like a cartoon Indian. the dust goes right through your clothes—locked up my wallet and watch, and went to find the shower.

It was a pretty crude arrangement, but it worked. Just a wooden floor with plywood walls, and water dripping down from a discarded jet fuel tank overhead, the kind that goes on the wing-tip. I wondered what had happened to the rest of the jet. There were twelve or thirteen guys standing shoulder-to-shoulder under the tank, scrubbing like mad. When one of them popped out I squeezed into his place. Then I found out why everyone was in such a hurry—the water was freezing! I lathered up, rinsed off, and jumped out, my teeth chattering. While I was drying myself, one of the guys waiting in line for the shower spoke up.

"Seems pretty cold, doesn't it?"

"Like ice water!"

"Man, it's not that cold. Just that your blood's gettin' thin. It's livin' in the tropics that does it. I've been here a week, and if I wasn't so fuckin' cruddy you couldn't *pay* me to get under that thing."

"That's great. That's really great."

"Well, they're supposed to heat it—see that little oil burner underneath the tank? Whoever's in charge of it's been slackin' off—we got hot water one time this week. And it didn't last long."

I got dry and walked back to the billet, walking carefully so as not to stir up dust onto my clean skin. The sun was setting, and I had to admit it looked real pretty. We had good sunsets in Oklahoma, too, but nothing like this;

bright splashes of crimson and purple just glowing in the dark sky. Must have been all the dust in the air.

Back in Basic, somebody had told me that Vietnam used to be a vacation spot for rich Europeans. I guess it *would* look pretty nice if you got rid of all the barbed wire and guns and mickey-mouse army shacks. While I was getting dressed I tried to picture what Cam Ranh Bay would look like with the army gone . . . suntanned dolls in bikinis, fat old rich men sitting under beach umbrellas with frosty tropical drinks, speedboats pulling water skiers through the bay . . . weird.

With a brand-new uniform, I felt like a human being again. It was ten minutes to six—1750 if you want to get technical—so I gathered up my comic books and went off to wait for the club to open.

I waited about half an hour—nothing good ever starts on time in the army—and this rough-looking master sergeant walked up to unlock the place.

"Ain't none of you guys comin' in here without you got yer canteen, yer pistol belt, yer first-aid pack, and yer steel pot. So jus' high-tail it back to yer billet an' get yer stuff straight.

"What you gonna do if ol' Charlie, he decides to hit tonight while yer in there gettin' drunk? You gonna stroll back t'yer billet and get yer stuff? No, you ain't. You gonna carry it with you all the time.

"And soljer, get them sleeves rolled down. Ev'y day at 1700 you gotta roll yer sleeves down cuz that's when the skeeters come out. One o' them malaria skeeters bites you and yer gonna wish you had that sleeve down.

"Them comic books ain't gonna keep the frags outa yer head, soljer. Go on back and getcher stuff."

I went back to the billet, feeling kind of stupid, and got out my stuff. I fastened the first-aid packet and the canteen to the pistol belt, rolled it all up and stuffed it in the steel pot. After all, he didn't say we had to *wear* the junk.

The beer was fairly cool. Somebody had managed to get some ice. The club was just a shack, but they actually had a juke box. I listened to the music for a while, reading my comics. Then a guy sat down across from me, dropping his helmet on the concrete floor with a loud clatter. "You're a new guy too, aren't ya?" he asked.

"Sure . . . how can you tell?"

"Take a look around. We're the only ones in here carryin' *this* shit around." He gave the helmet a kick. "They say this is the safest place in the whole fuckin' Central Highlands."

"Well, that's good to hear."

"Yeah." He stuck out his hand. "Willy Horowitz."

"Farmer, John Farmer. Just come in today?"

"Yeah, same plane as you, I think." He sucked down about half the can of beer. "What you do, back in the world?"

"Nothin' much. Just got out of school last June. Pumped gas for a few months, then got a job typing at the courthouse in Enid. Oklahoma."

"Didn't wanta go to college?"

"Thought about it—didn't have the grades to get a scholarship, though. Said the hell with it. How 'bout you?"

"I went for a year. City College, New York—guess I partied too much, flunked chemistry and got kicked out, for half a year, anyhow. Plenty of time to get drafted—you didn't *join up*, did you?"

"Hell, no. All I did was turn nineteen."

"Where'd you do Basic?"

"Fort Leonard Wood. That's in—"

"Yeah, I know, Missouri. Asshole of the world. I got my Engineer training there."

"Me, too," I said. "Bet we were there about the same time."

"Our cycle got out the end of December."

"Same here—what company?"

"Bravo."

"How 'bout that—I was in Charlie. We were practically next-door neighbors."

"I'll drink to that . . . hell, I'll drink to anything." He crunched the beer can double and stood up. "Ready for another?"

"Yeah—here." I pushed a dollar at him.

"Shit, keep it. I been playin' poker, got more damn MPC's than I know what to do with."

MPC's, Military Payment Certificates, were what everybody used for money in Vietnam. They had different colored bills for tens, fives, and ones, then little bills like Monopoly money instead of coins. You could buy slugs at the bar, to operate the juke box.

"Budweiser OK?" He had two cans in each hand, set them down in the middle of the table.

"Sure." I slid one over and sipped it. "How do you like it so far?"

"Like it?"

"The war, Vietnam."

"Shit." He took out a cigarette and tapped it on his thumbnail. "It wouldn't be so bad . . . you know, armywise. They don't hassle you like they did Stateside—but God, that rocket attack—were you in Cam Ranh Bay when—"

"Yeah, that was bad."

"Bad . . . scared me shitless. Wonder how often, how much of that shit we're gonna get."

"Don't know," I said. "Guy told me that was just a picnic compared to the real thing."

"Yeah, but ya never know. Some guys like to act hardcore, scare the shit out of ya."

"Guess we just wait and see."

"Yeah." He looked at his watch. "Look, there's a movie on in a few minutes, outside by the billet . . . wanna go check it out?"

"Sure." We got a good supply of beer and split.

It was pitch dark on the way over, and I managed to step into a ditch. They had these three-foot-deep ditches all over the area; you're supposed to dive into one when the shooting starts. I turned my ankle and limped the rest of the way to the movie.

It was one of those Italian-made Westerns, about some guys blowing up a bridge. Pretty good.

When they turned off the movie it was almost pitch-black—just a little bit of starlight—but we had pretty much figured out where the ditches were. Managed to get back to our bunks without breaking my neck.

It had gotten right cool and I didn't have any trouble falling asleep. But I don't think I slept more than a few minutes when some guy pulled on my leg, nearly yanking me out of bed.

"Incoming! We got incoming!" Then I could hear the faint *crump—crump*, just like it'd been in Cam Ranh Bay a few days before. I jumped down, scooped my steel pot off the floor, and ran for the door. It was a mess, everybody trying to get out at once. I finally got outside and ran for the nearest ditch. Cut my bare foot on a rock but hardly felt it. I jumped into the ditch and laid down lengthways.

You could hear the rockets whistling in, but you couldn't see them. The explosions got louder and louder. My throat got dry and I started shaking.

Then a bright blue flash and the ground jumped, and a noise like somebody slapped your ear with a baseball bat. It must have been real close; you could smell the smoke and hear clods of dirt falling out of the sky.

Someone down at the end of the ditch yelled, "Medic! Jesus Christ—Medic! I been hit!" The medic ran by me, out of the ditch, crouched low. Another round whistled in and the medic jumped in the ditch, but it landed pretty far away. He got back out and ran down to the wounded guy. Watching him, I decided there were worse things than being a combat engineer.

"Pass it down!" The guy on my left handed me an M 16. I gave it to the next guy and told him to pass it down. I passed about twenty of them and then got one for myself. It wasn't loaded. I remembered the sergeant saying he'd bring ammo if there was going to be trouble. But I wondered whether he'd actually come from wherever he was, with rockets dropping all around. I knew I wouldn't.

The attack lasted about fifteen minutes. None of the other rounds came as close as that one. They told us to stay in the ditch—there could be another attack any time. That was all right with me at first—I felt pretty safe where I was—but after a while I was ready to get out and take my chances. I was just wearing the shorts I slept in, and it was cold. I was also grimy from lying in the ditch and my foot throbbed where I'd cut it on the rock.

We must have laid there for hours. Finally they told us to get out and turn in the guns. I went and washed off my foot. It didn't look bad, but it sure hurt like the dickens. I found the medic and he bandaged it for me.

About dawn they said we could turn in. They said we could have two extra hours of sack time—get up at 0800 —and acted like they were doing us a favor. I could have used two extra *days*, but I was too tired to complain. My head hit the pillow and I was out.

CHAPTER THREE

I thought I'd been dirty before, but the next morning when they rolled us out of bed, I was caked and crawly-feeling with red grime. Sleeping on it kind of grinds it in.

Decided to skip breakfast and take a shower, but the water was all gone by the time I got there. So I got dressed and headed for the chow hall. The food was all gone, of course. I got a cup of coffee that tasted like diesel fuel. It woke me up a little, but I still felt like I'd had only two hours' sleep after cowering in a ditch all night.

Refilled my canteen cup with coffee and dumped enough sugar in it to kill the taste, then carried it back to our billet. It was 0845; we didn't have to report for training until 0900.

I sat on a pile of sandbags and watched the people mill around. There was a line of about fifty guys doing a police call, walking in a straight line picking up cigarette butts and such. They seemed more interested in it than usual (usually you just walk along looking at the ground, picking up something when you think someone's watching). A couple of them were really excited, showing off their finds to each other. What's so interesting about a cigarette butt?

The coffee was making me sick, so I tossed out the last half-cup of it. Where it splashed, I saw a glistening piece of metal.

That's what they were picking up. I brushed the dust off the thing and looked at it. Everybody'd talked about shrapnel in Basic—it's the stuff that causes the most casualties—but this was the first actual piece of it that I'd ever seen. It was a chunk of lead about an inch square with razor-sharp edges. I handled it carefully, but it still made a little nick on my finger. It looked like it could go right through a person without slowing down.

Here in 'Nam they called them "frags" instead of shrapnel. That's what they were—fragments—like when an artillery shell goes off, the explosive inside shatters the lead casing into hundreds of frags.

This one must have been one of the frags that had been whistling over my head last night. I wrapped it up in a scrap of paper and put it in my shirt pocket.

They were lining up in front of the billet, so I walked over to join in the fun.

"Awright, listen up." Old Sergeant O'Donnell stepped in front with a clipboard in his hand. "Today yer lucky. We just gotta go across the street for half-a-day's training. I know you guys didn't get much sleep last night. Tough shit. Neither did I. Anybody falls asleep, he goes on KP tomorrow morning." Some of the guys looked like they couldn't stay awake in the middle of a rock band.

We marched more or less in step to a bunch of wooden benches across the street. Whoever was supposed to teach us hadn't showed up yet—probably getting some sleep!—so I just sat down and smoked to stay awake.

"Why the fuck did we have to get a master sergeant?" Willy slumped down next to me on the bench and lit a cigarette. "He's gonna be nothin' but trouble."

"Maybe every bunch has to have one."

"Fuck, no—billet next to ours has a corporal in charge."

The sergeant came back with a captain walking in front of him. O'Donnell looked at us flopped around on the benches and yelled, "Tench-hut, goddammit!" We came to attention in a creaky sort of way.

"At ease, men." The captain waved a hand in our general direction. "Sit down. Smoke if you want to.

"I'm Captain Price, Artillery, here to tell you how the

28

army uses artillery to support the infantry in the field. Any artillery boys in the crowd?" A couple of hands went up. "Well, you two might just as well close your eyes and get some sleep—if you don't know everything I'm tellin' these guys, and more besides, your ass is grass anyhow.

"You were supposed to get instruction on the .45 automatic this morning, from Sergeant Something or other. But one of the rocket rounds last night hit the shed where we keep all the demonstration .45's—so you're just gonna have to learn about that on your own, if you get issued a .45. Doesn't make any difference to me one way or the other, of course, except that you'll get off two hours earlier, and I had to get up two hours earlier to give you my talk. I know that just breaks you up." Even Willy chuckled. Captain Price seemed to be all right, for an officer.

"Artillery comes in two varieties, ours and theirs. Either one can kill you dead. All you have to do is be standing in a spot where a frag wants to go.

"Jungle warfare's almost always close range. You grunts, you infantrymen, are going to have Charlie so close you'll be able to smell his BO." People laughed. "I'm not kidding! And even when he's that close, you'll be having artillery dropped in on him, and be damned glad it's there, too. Otherwise, he might be in your foxhole with a knife.

"When it's coming down right in front of you like that, just keep your head down and you'll be OK. Most of these rounds could fall a few meters away; if you're scrunched down in a foxhole you won't get hurt.

"Of course, maybe one time in a hundred, in a thousand, that round's gonna fall short and land right in your lap. Don't waste time worryin' about that. If it happens, you won't feel a thing.

"Now, we have several kinds of artillery, broken down according to how big around the shell is. Biggest one is the eight-incher . . ."

He went on for about an hour, telling about the different

kinds of artillery, their "kill radius," how fast they can shoot, and such. I don't think I remembered a tenth of it.

We had a break for coffee and then piled onto an open truck. It took us about a mile, to Camp Enari's perimeter. We got off and stood around while Captain Price talked into a hand radio, getting clearance to drop a few shells into the valley below us.

"Now these 105's will be about the smallest rounds you'll see in combat, not counting the mortars. First comes the smoke round—watch!"

There was a ragged, rustling sound, then a distant pop (the sound of the gun catching up with the shell), and a louder pop, then a puff of white smoke in the jungle below.

"Drop fifty and fire three HE," the captain said into the microphone. I could remember that meant to crank the gun down so it would aim fifty meters closer, and shoot three HE, high explosive, rounds.

"Now look at that little clearing down there." The rustle was much louder than before, followed by pop-pop-pop, and the clearing exploded in three fountains of dirt and gray smoke. The noise of the explosions was loud rolling thunder.

"Well, that's the show, boys. Wish you could see more, but we can't spare the ammunition." He got into his jeep, "Want a ride back, Sergeant?" Our truck had already left.

"Yes, *sir*— Specialist, you march these people back to the billet." They left in a cloud of dust.

"All right, quit bitchin'." The guy was a specialist fourth class, a Spec/4; not quite a sergeant. "At least that's all we're gonna do today. We can go back and hit the sack."

"You ain't gonna make us march, are ya, Specialist?" That was Willy.

"Hell, no. We'll just walk down to the main road and see if we can catch a ride—but fer Chrissake don't forget to salute everything that moves!"

It was a couple of blocks to the road. We stood there for half an hour (long enough to walk it, actually), breathing dust and saluting every couple of minutes, until an empty dump truck pulled up and hauled us to the Admin area.

The specialist advised us to fade out of sight; there was bound to be somebody cruising around looking for detail men. 'Most everybody hiked up to the PX, but I was too tired. Decided to take my chances and headed straight for the sack. It took me about three seconds to fall asleep.

"What the *fuck* do y'think yer doin', soljer?" I looked up bleary-eyed and saw three stripes. Buck-sergeant.

"Just gettin' a little shut-eye, Sarge. Training's over for the day."

"Trainin' might be over, but work ain't over. Yer on my sandbag detail."

"I'm not even in your platoon, Sarge."

"What, you givin' me lip, soljer? Wanna see the Captain?"

I knew when I was licked. I sat up and tried to shake the sleep out of my head. "Where's your fuckin' detail?"

"That's more like it. Follow me." We walked out of the billet into the blazing sun. Four men with their shirts off were sitting on a pile of sandbags.

"Awright, goddammit, get to work. Nobody leaves 'til you fill ev'ry fuckin' one of those bags."

I took off my own shirt and joined the group. The sergeant walked off, and a wiry little colored guy handed me a gray burlap sack. Seemed like every other guy in Vietnam was Negro.

"Here, you hold for a while. I'll dig."

"Suits." I held the bag open and he dumped a shovelful of dirt into it. "How'd you get on this detail?"

"Same as these other guys. We got some Cokes at the Class-Six store and came back to drink 'em—found a nice cool bunker, then that asshole of a buck-sergeant found us."

"Yeah," said another guy with an Alabama drawl, "This fuckin' army—we gotta spend all day fillin' sandbags we'll never get t'use."

"I don't know," I said. "We might be behind 'em tonight."

"Might. Might not. How'd he get aholt of you?"

"Just tryin' to get some sleep."

The Alabama boy kicked his shovel in deep and leaned on it. "This goddamn fuckin' army. Charlie keeps ya awake all night and the fuckin' sergeants won't let ya catch up in the day."

It went on like that for several hours. We wound up putting empty sandbags inside the ones we were filling—otherwise we never would've gotten through. Guess it was about four when we put the shovels back in a shed and went our separate ways. I was going to hide somewhere and catch a nap, but first I checked the billet. There were a dozen guys snoring away inside, so I said the hell with it and went to my bunk and flopped. I didn't even wake up for chow.

The next morning we went out to a rifle range and learned how to use an M-16. Some of the guys had them in Basic Training, but most of us hadn't ever shot one before. The stock and grip are hollow fiber glass, so the gun's really light, as light as my .22 at home. But it can really shoot 'em up—put the selector on AUTO and hold down the trigger, and eighteen bullets come out all at once. We learned how to zero them in so the bullets went about where you aimed, and spent the rest of the time murdering tin cans.

In the afternoon we learned how to use explosives. That was kind of interesting, since, being a combat engineer, I'm supposed to know all about them. But I was on KP all the time we'd studied explosives in training, so it was all new.

"These are the things you're gonna be using most often." The guy teaching the class was a Spec/5 not much older than me.

"TNT." He held up a block about half the size of a brick, covered with green paper.

"C-4 plastic explosive." It looked like an overgrown piece of taffy, a white rubbery stick about a foot long.

"Det cord, detonation cord." Looked just like plastic clothesline.

"Time fuse." Looked like the det cord, but orange.

"And, of course, blasting caps." Skinny silver tube.

"Mostly you're gonna use the C-4, because the TNT doesn't work too well if it gets wet. And everything gets wet during the monsoon season.

"Now here's all you have to do, to make a big noise. First you take the crimpers"—he held up a funny-looking pair of pliers—"and crimp a blasting cap onto some fuse." He blew in the end of the cap and slipped a length of fuse into it. Then he squeezed the end of the cap with the jaws of the crimpers, and gave it a couple of tugs to show that it was securely fastened to the fuse.

"Now when you get out in the field you're gonna see hard-core engineers crimp these caps with their teeth, like in the movies. If you're *real* lucky you might see one of them get his jaw blown off. Don't do it.

"In all this bag of tricks," he waved an arm at the pile of various explosives behind him, "the only things really dangerous to *you* are the blasting caps. The rest of it, you can burn or shoot full of holes, nothin's gonna happen.

"But drop one of these blasting caps on the sidewalk—if you can find a sidewalk—and you'll be lookin' for a new pair of balls.

"Now to put the cap in the C-4"—he broke off a piece of C-4 a few inches long—"you just punch a hole in it with the pointy ended handle of the crimpers. The other handle's a screwdriver, which you'll never use.

"Make the hole about as deep as the cap and push the cap in. Like this. Now follow me." He led us over to a hole in the ground, big enough to hide a truck in. He set the piece of C-4 inside the edge of the hole.

"Let me use your cigarette." He took a cigarette from a guy and touched it to the fuse and blew on it. "You can use matches, but a cigarette works better."

The fuse started to sputter and he said calmly, "Get away and get down." I ran like hell, not knowing whether to expect a firecracker or an H-bomb.

"That's far enough," he shouted. I hit the dirt and the thing went bang, a little louder than a rifle. We went back and sat down again.

"Most of you prob'ly won't ever use this stuff. Explosives are the engineers' job. But you've all gotta know how to do it in case of an emergency, like all your engineers getting killed." Oh yeah.

"You almost never use these things as weapons—you've got plenty of explosives made for that purpose. Mostly you use the C-4 for blowing down trees, either to make an LZ—helicopter landing zone—or to clear away enough of the jungle so that Charlie can't come too close without you seeing him.

"You don't want to blow down your trees one by one, so you use the det cord to make all the charges go off at once.

"This stuff"—he held up a coil of the white cord—"is nothing more than hollow plastic tubing filled with an explosive similar to C-4. If something goes bang at one end, the bang travels down the cord to the other end. To make sure everything goes off all at once, you ought to put a cap on each end of the det cord. But in a pinch, you can just wrap it around the explosive a few times."

He used the det cord to string together a bunch of different kinds of explosives, to show us where the caps went in each one. There were cratering charges, a Bangalore torpedo, a Claymore mine, a dynamite stick, and a number of other things that I never saw again. At the end of the session, he blew the whole thing up. Even scrunched down in a foxhole a block away, it was so loud it made my ears hurt. They rang all the next day.

The week went by pretty fast. We learned about weapons, booby traps, jungle survival—even spent a night out in Charlie's Country, on the other side of the barbed wire. Nothing happened, but it was spooky.

It was like Basic Training all over again, but boiled down and concentrated and with all the bullshit taken out. In Basic they treated you as if you were a boy, and a moron at that—but there's no room for tots or stupids in the jungle.

When the week was over, they posted lists telling where everybody was assigned. Willy and I both drew B Company, Fourth Engineers.

CHAPTER FOUR

The supply sergeant just looked at us when we walked into the supply room, stood there behind the counter and looked at us without saying anything. He rolled a dead cigar butt from one side of his mouth to the other, and back again.

"New guys." It wasn't a question.

"Yes, I'm—"

"Lemme see a couple copies of yer orders." We handed them over.

"Farmer, Horowitz." He took the cigar out of his mouth and looked at Willy. "Joosh?"

"Huh?"

"You Joosh or what?"

"Oh. Yeah, I'm a Jew. What about it?"

"Lucky sumbitch." He shuffled the papers around.

"Lucky?"

"Yeah, we gotta let ya go t' Long Binh fer those crazy holidays. No synagogue around here.

"Had a Joosh guy till a coupla months ago. Useta go to Long Binh for a coupla days an' come back really fucked up. Lucky sumbitch."

He got out two copies of a list titled "COMBAT IS-SUE—B Company, Fourth Engineers." At the bottom there was a place for your name. He printed our names in the blanks, slowly and carefully.

"Says here plain as day, 'please print,' but none o' you

fuckers c'n read so you just put some squiggly fuckin' line that's s'posed to be yer name. So *I* gotta write it.

"Okay." He started at the top of the list. "Rifle, M-16, Serial number such-and-such." He clumped over to a rifle rack, unlocked it, and pulled out the first two M-16s.

"Take good care o' these." He tossed them on the counter with a plastic-sounding clatter. "Gon' save yer life some day."

He slapped two pens on the counter. "Serial number's on th' enda th' barrel. Write it inna blank."

He put his finger on the second item on the list. "Ammunition, 5.63mm, 100 rounds. You don't get none o' that."

"No ammo?" I said.

"Tha's right. Otherwise you fuckers get drunk an' start shootin' each other in th' ass—"

"Then what the hell are we going to do in case of an attack?" Willy was indignant.

"Son, I been here goin' on twenty-one months—"

"You came back?" I couldn't believe *anybody* would spend more than a year here.

"Shit, yeah. Twenty-one months, like I say, an' I ain't once had to shoot my M-16. Don' even know if th' fucker works." He put a finger on his chin and frowned. "Hey, jus' a second.

"HEY, FUCKFACE!" he yelled.

"Yeah, Sarge," came a tired voice from a back room.

"Where them fuckin' manifests come in this mornin'?"

"Second drawer down on your right. Where I always put—"

"None o' yer fuckin' lip, Private." He opened the drawer and fished out two little tickets.

"Yeah, you get ammo. Yer shippin' out in th' mornin'." He went back to the gun rack, unloaded a box, and brought back two cartons of ammunition. Then he added four hand grenades.

"The rest o' this shit, we already got made up." He pointed to two big plastic bags, the kind laundries use, standing up in a corner. They were filled with various objects, mostly green.

He turned the lists around so we could read them. "That oughta be it."

The rest of the list went like this:

1 BANDOLIER
1 HELMET, STEEL
1 LINER, HELMET
1 NET, CAMOUFLAGE
1 BAR, MOSQUITO
2 JACKETS, FATIGUE, JUNGLE
2 TROUSERS, FATIGUE, JUNGLE
2 UNDERSHIRTS, GREEN
2 DRAWERS, GREEN
1 BOOTS, TROPICAL, PROTECTIVE SOLE, PAIR
4 SOCKS, GREEN, PAIR
1 PACKFRAME, ALUMINUM
1 RUCKSACK
1 PONCHO
1 LINER, PONCHO
1 MATTRESS, AIR
1 PACKET, FIRST-AID
1 BELT, PISTOL
2 GRENADES, HAND FRAGMENTATION
1 BAYONET
2 CANTEENS, FIBER GLASS, GREEN

"What are we supposed to *do* with all this crap?" Willy asked.

"Do with it? Lemme see." He looked at the list. "Well, y'carry the gun. Stuff the ammo in the bandolier and sling it across yer chest, like a Mexican bandit. Put the liner in the helmet and the camouflage net over the helmet and dump it all on yer head. Put the bayonet and the first-aid packet on the pistol belt and hang it on yer hips. Then buckle the rucksack on the packframe and stuff everything else into the rucksack. Got it?"

"Then you put the rucksack on your back and try to walk. Right?"

The sergeant laughed. "You poor fucker. Son, that ain't

thirty pounds worth of stuff. Wait'll you get out in the field and they give you a week's worth of C-rations and 200 more rounds of ammo. Lemme see, and a carton of butts and ten pounds of C-4 and an ax and a few more grenades—when you go back to the world you'll have the strongest back on the block.

"Anyhow, I'll show you how to put the rucksack on the packframe. Get everything together tonight—you're leavin' bright an' early tomorrow for Ban Me Thuot. You oughta take shavin' gear and stationery, but leave the rest of your personal shit here, in your footlocker. Remember, everything goes on your back."

We managed to get the stuff together and staggered out to where the supply sergeant said the billets were. *Had* to be more than thirty pounds!

I had a pretty good night's sleep, but it was still dark when a guy came in with a flashlight and shook us awake.

"Farmer and Horowitz? Saddle up—there's a jeep waiting for you outside." The guy smoked a cigarette in the darkness while Willy and I dressed.

"Who're you?" I asked.

"Masters, PFC Masters. I'm the supply clerk."

"Don't suppose you need another supply clerk . . . or anything clerk."

"Nah. We got clerks out the ass in this company. You oughta be glad you don't hafta stick around here and put up with all the bullshit." He ground his cigarette out on the floor. "Yeah, I kinda envy you guys. Out where the action is."

"Trade you all the action for your typewriter," I said.

"Man, you don't *know*—half the guys out there go all year without ever gettin' shot at. Just sit on their butts an' take it easy. Free cigarettes, lotsa beer, Red Cross broads . . ."

"Still trade. Somebody's gettin' shot. I'd just as soon it was somebody else."

He lit another cigarette. "Yeah. Guess I could get reassigned to combat if I really wanted to. Think about it, too, every time the supply sergeant gets a bug up his ass."

I heard Willy grunt as he hoisted the pack. "Ready to move out, Willy?"

"Ready as I'll ever be. Still asleep, though, goddammit."

By the time the jeep got to Pleiku it was getting light. Masters suggested we should poke our guns out the window, just in case, as we drove through. We did, but nobody paid much attention to us.

When we got out of the jeep, Masters handed us a manifest, a plane ticket, to Ban Me Thuot. I took it into the little stucco building by the airstrip, and the guy at the desk told us it'd be loading in another hour or so. We sat and wrote letters until he called us.

The pilot of the C-130 made us leave our hand grenades behind—the supply sergeant should have known they wouldn't allow them on the plane—and we had about a half-hour's ride to a run-down airstrip in Ban Me Thuot. The strip was full of holes, filled with gravel.

There was a sign on the airstrip INCOMING FOURTH DIVISION PERSONNEL REPORT TO FOURTH DIVISION TRAINS AREA. That was us, but neither of us had any idea what the hell a "trains" area was. There were a bunch of tents at the end of the airstrip, so we headed for them. It turned out that the whole shmear, about a hundred tents, was the trains area. We wandered around for a while—nobody else in sight—'til I finally stuck my head in a tent and some sergeant gave us directions to the engineer's outfit. He was shaving, looked like he'd just gotten up.

"This place don't look too fuckin' dangerous," Willy said as we walked down the dirt road.

"What do you think made those holes in the airstrip—termites?"

"Well, yeah. Still, you don't see anybody gettin' ready to fight a war."

"I don't see anybody at *all.* It's only seven o'clock—maybe they don't fight until after lunch."

"That must be the place." Willy pointed at a tent with a

sign that had the Fourth Division cloverleaf and said ENGIN. B CO. We went into the tent.

Inside, there was a guy asleep in a chair in front of a radio set. Willy went over and shook his arm. "Hey, fella, wake up."

He sat up straight and looked around. "Jesus Christ—was I asleep?" He looked at his watch. "Captain'd have my ass in a sling . . . thanks. Who are you guys, anyhow?"

"I'm Willy Horowitz and this is John Farmer. New guys."

"Just two? They said five or six . . . you just get in?"

" 'Bout fifteen minutes ago."

"Hey, do me a favor, the mess tent's just across the street. Get us some coffee, OK?"

"Sure," Willy went out the flap.

"Take off your pack and have a seat. I gotta find the papers for you guys."

I sat down and took out a cigarette, decided to wait and smoke it with my coffee. "How is it out here?"

"Here? Oh, pretty much like base camp. Not as much spit-'n-polish. Three hots a day and beer at night, if we're lucky. Only had two attacks all the time I've been here. Nobody hurt."

"Sounds pretty good."

"Oh, it is—hell of a lot better than where *you're* goin'."

"We aren't gonna stay here?"

"Nah, you're goin' out to either Brillo Pad or, uh, two-one-two-four."

"Where's that?"

"Hills nearby. Fire bases."

"Fire bases. So what's a fire base?"

"Man, a *fire* base. That's where they keep the big guns, artillery. Safest place in the world, forty, fifty big guns and mortars, two grunt companies—two hundred men, man, no way Charlie's gonna fuck around with you. That's a fire base."

"How come one has a name and the other has a number?"

"Oh, the number *is* the name—the 'two' means infantry;

'21' means A Company and '24' means D Company, that's the two infantry companies on the hill."

Willy came back with the coffee. It tasted terrible.

A tall man, the first guy I'd seen with creases in his pants, came into the tent. "Morning, David."

"Morning, Captain." Willy and I started to come to attention but saw that the guy at the radio stayed in his seat. We stood up anyhow.

He grabbed my hand while I was still deciding whether to salute. "I'm Cap'n Brown, your company commander." He shook hands with Willy, too. "You must be replacements—where are the others, getting chow?"

"Uh, sir, we're the only ones they sent."

He bit his lower lip and picked up a clipboard. "I see. What're your names?"

We told him. "Yes, you're on this list. But so are four others." He sat down on the table and leafed through the papers. "We're under strength. 'Way under. Those Goddern base camp commandos. We need men out here for *soldier* work—and they grab half our replacements for permanent KP and paper-shuffling."

Why couldn't I have been one of those lucky four? I can wash a mean dish.

"Well, you-all go get some breakfast. Then get a couple of cases of beer from the mess sergeant and head out to the helicopter pad. Tell the pad man to put you on a slick to 2124."

Breakfast wasn't too awful, but we had to go back and get a note from the captain before the mess sergeant would give us any beer.

The pad was quite a ways from the trains area. That case of beer was getting mighty heavy by the time we got there.

No helicopters, just a bunch of supplies lying around, and the dirtiest guy I'd ever seen, sitting on a crate, drinking beer.

"You the pad man?"

"Nah, he went to get some chow." He gave us the once-over. "New guys?"

"Yeah." I said, "Bravo Company engineers."

"You won't be clean again for a long time. Better enjoy it while you can—pull up a box and crack a beer."

It sounded like a good idea. He let us use his church key. It was on a chain around his neck, all wrapped up in green tape. His dog tags were wrapped the same way; I asked about it.

"That's so they won't jingle, man. You gotta be quiet. Don' want to jingle in the jungle." He laughed, a dry cackle. "Where you two goin'?"

"Place called 2124."

"2124? Oh yeah—2124!" He cackled again. "That's where I'm headed, too—but that's not what we call it."

"Place has a name?"

"Yeah." Cackle, cackle.

"Alamo. Alamo Hill."

CHAPTER FIVE

The first "slick"—that's a helicopter big enough to hold six people—was headed for the Alamo. He didn't even shut off the engine; we three just piled in and he lifted off again.

The bird was equipped with sliding doors for both walls, and both of them were open (imagine riding in a convertible going 100 miles an hour, a half-mile up in the air). Door gunners were strapped on either side, leaning on .30 caliber machine guns. They looked bored. The pilot and co-pilot looked bored. I was scared shitless.

After about fifteen minutes we dropped down to treetop level and roared up the side of a hill. It was green bamboo jungle all the way up to the top, and all of a sudden, dirt—Alamo, a brown scab covering the mountaintop. Barbed wire and bunkers. Heavy artillery all over. On a low-level patch not much bigger than the helicopter, a guy was waving his arms. The helicopter set down gently and kept roaring away, kicking up dust while we helped unload two flame throwers, a mailbag, and lots of C-rations.

So I got my first good look at a fire base through a cloud of whirling dust, dry sticks, and bits of paper kicked up by the helicopter blades. Most people do, I guess.

First, it was really filthy. Everything and everybody was covered with that reddish dust. It had a temporary look; no buildings except for a couple of steel tocks that were probably dropped in by helicopter. I guessed people lived in the bunkers, holes in the ground with crude log roofs piled high with sandbags.

The artillery pieces were clean, black metal shiny with oil, and I could see why; half the crews seemed busy wiping rags over the metal. Looked to be about 20 real artillery-type guns, plus another dozen mortars, each one a black stovepipe about waist-high.

There wasn't any order to the place; the bunkers seemed to be just scattered around all over the hill. The guns were all together in one place, though, and so were the mortars.

Finally the slick lifted and fell away, down the side of the hills. Everything was eery quiet, like cotton stuffed in your ears.

Speaking, I realized I was more than half deaf from the noise. "Hey, buddy," I asked the pad man, "where do the engineers hang out around here?"

He pointed up the hill to what looked like a wooden shack on wheels, with a tattered American flag fluttering above it.

"If you swallow hard a couple of times, you'll be able to hear OK," Willy said. I did and it worked.

Right by the shack (which turned out to be a trailer with walls and a roof built over it), there were four guys digging a hole and filling sandbags.

"This Bravo Company engineers?"

An old guy, about thirty-five, dropped his shovel and climbed out of the hole. "That's us." He stuck out his hand. "Sergeant Pobanovitch, call me Pop. Which of you is Farmer and which is Horowitz?"

We got straightened out and he introduced us to the others. "The tall one's Doc Jones, the medic." Jones was the only Negro in the bunch. "Guy with the pick is Fats— Fats, what the hell is your real name?"

"Don't matter. Fats is OK."

"And I'm John Williamson," the last one said. "They call me Professor." He *looked* kind of like a professor, too; horn-rimmed glasses and bald halfway up his head. But he was just as dirty as the rest, and unshaven to boot.

"All right, men, take a break," Pop said. "We'll help you get rid of some of that beer."

"Yeah, it's lunchtime anyhow."

"You ever think about anything else, Fats?"

"You betcher sweet ass I do!" He went over to a cardboard box and fished out a green tin can. "None of them around, though."

"Let me show you guys how to eat C's," the Professor said. He pulled out three C-ration cans and started opening one with a P-38 Army issue miniature can opener. "You don't want to open it all the way—leave enough so you can use the top as a handle." He bent the top over so it made a kind of messy handle. "Then you find yourself a stove, like this." He picked up another tin can with both ends removed to make a hollow stand, with holes punched in the side. "Now. You take some C-4"—he took a stick of the white plastic explosive out of his pocket—"pinch off a piece the size of a marble, put it in the stove and light it." It flared up with an orange flame, and he put the C-ration can on top of the stove. "It heats up real fast but you've got to stir like mad to keep it from burning on the bottom."

The can he brought over for me turned out to be frankfurters and beans; Willy got spaghetti and meatballs. Not bad. For dessert, we opened cans of fruit.

"Farmer, you and Horowitz are going out with the Prof tomorrow to relieve the engineer squad with A Company, First of the Twelfth. Prof'll be in charge, and your squad's code name is Two-One-X-ray. That's what we'll call over the radio when we want to talk to you.

"Reminds me—we've gotta get code names for both of you. Can't use real names over the air. Either of you have a nickname?"

I remembered Smitty at Cam Ranh Bay. "Anything but Tex. Call me Okie."

"Okie it is." Pop wrote it down in a little notebook. "Horowitz?"

He puffed on his cigarette. "Hmm . . . how 'bout 'Whore'?"

"Fine." He wrote it down. "Now—good thing you came

so early; didn't think we'd get this bunker done by night-fall. Fats, you get a chain saw and Doc, get an ax; go out an' get us some overhead. Rest of us'll keep digging here. Including the lieutenant, if he ever gets back from that goddamn meeting."

"Meetin'!" Doc snorted. "You *know* they's up there drinkin' beer and tellin' dirty stories. Lieutenant's not comin' back 'til the work's all done."

" 'RHIP' Doc—remember what that means?"

"Yeah . . . 'rank has its privileges'—too many fuckin' privileges, if y' ask me."

"So who asked you? Take a couple of beers, but don't let any officers see you drinkin' on the other side of the perimeter. If they do, I'll swear I don't know where you got 'em."

"OK, Pop." Doc put a beer in his leg pocket and tossed one to Fats.

"Also, don't fuck around out there, y'hear? Get *big* logs—you two're gonna be stayin' in this bunker."

"We know, Pop," Fats said. "The life you save . . ."

". . . may be your own. Goddamn right." Pop watched them gather up their tools and start down the hill, then turned to us.

"So that's the way we run things around here. Free an' easy, no bullshit. Long as everybody follows orders. Any-body starts to fuck around, we lean on him. I lean on him. The lieutenant leans on him. And life can get pretty sorry. Understand?"

We both nodded. "OK—Farmer, get on the pick for a while, break up the ground in the bottom of the hole. Horowitz, shovel the dirt onto that pile. Me an' Prof'll fill sandbags."

I picked away for half an hour and my palms started to blister. Willy traded with me, and the shovel seemed to put blisters everywhere the pick hadn't. After an hour we took a break for a beer.

"Pop," I said. "how dangerous is it out in the field? Many engineers get hurt?"

"No, not many. Too many, but not many compared to the

infantry . . . you'll be part of the 'command group,' always in the middle, infantry all around you."

"It's like this," the Professor added. "The company moves through the jungle in three lines, right flank, left flank, and center file. We'll be in the middle of the center file. Charlie's got to get through a flank before he can get to us."

"But sometimes he does," Willy said.

"Sometimes." The Prof took a big swig of beer. "And sometimes he pops mortars or rifle grenades into the center file. But it's nothing like being on the line, smelling his breath."

"How often?" I asked.

"Hmm?"

"How often do you run into Charlie?"

"Oh, we make contact, what, about twice or three times a month, on the average. A Company hasn't made any contact in two weeks or so, now."

"Means they're due?" Willy asked.

"Doesn't mean anything, except they've been lucky for two weeks. Maybe they'll be lucky for two weeks more. Maybe for the rest of the year."

"Still sounds bad," Willy said.

"Ah, don't sweat it, Horowitz. I'm *glad* I'm goin' out in the field again. One heck of a lot safer than it is here— Alamo's been hit twice this week."

"Jesus Christ!"

"Not all that bad, just mortars. Couple of guys hurt, but nobody's been killed yet. They're bound to try a ground attack, though. I'd just as soon be someplace else when it comes." Prof wiped his forehead with a filthy rag.

"Ain't gonna be no fuckin' ground attack," Pop said.

"That's what they said on Brillo Pad, Pop."

"Tell y'what, Prof. Those Intelligence boys been sayin' we're gonna have a ground attack, three days in a row now. I'll bet you ten bucks there won't be an attack tonight, ten there won't be one Friday night, and ten there won't be one Saturday night."

"I'd hate to collect, Pop."

"You won't collect. Intelligence's got its head up its ass, as usual—hi, Lieutenant. How'd the meeting go?"

A guy not much older than me sat down on a pile of sandbags and took off his hat, wiped his forehead. "Same as usual, Pop. Except Intelligence—no attack tonight."

"Bet's off, Professor!" The Prof laughed.

"Lot mo guooo," the Lieutenant said. "You're Horowitz and you're, uh, Farmer."

"Sorry, sir. I'm Farmer and he's Horowitz."

"Glad you could make it. Another dozen and we'd be all set. Anybody got a butt?"

Pop threw him a pack of Winstons. He took out one and tossed it back. "Reminds me—we've got an SP pack down at the pad. Somebody wanta go get it?"

"On my way," Professor said.

"What's an SP pack?" Willy asked.

"Mostly cigarettes and candy," the lieutenant said. "Pop, you about ready to put overhead on this bunker?"

"Yeah, I've got Doc an' Fats on it."

"OK . . . what can I do besides drink one of those beers?"

"Thought we'd just take it easy until we get the overhead."

"Suits." He cracked a beer. "See, that's the way it is. I command this platoon, but Pop leads it. Pop, if I ordered you to eat a pile of shit, would you do it?"

"With a grin on my face, sir."

"I just bet you would. Anyhow, anything Pop says, goes. Anybody else tells you to do something, you can try to reason with him."

Doc and Fats came puffing up the hill, balancing two eight-foot logs on their shoulders. They dropped them by the hole and flopped down panting.

"Got six more this size," Doc said. "Afternoon, sir." Pant, pant. "How 'bout lettin' us take a break while the new guys haul up a couple?"

We got to our feet. "Just show us where they are," Willy said.

"I'll go with yuh," Doc said, getting up. "Oh, my achin' back."

"Give yourself a Darvon, Doc."

"Fuck, sir, I'll stick to aspirin. Let's go."

We found the logs, and Doc showed us how to get one on each shoulder. They didn't start to get heavy until we'd gone about ten steps. We barely made it to the top.

"Good job," Pop said. "OK, Fats, you an' Doc get the next two. Then Farmer and Horowitz again."

"What kind of cigarettes you smoke?" Prof was opening a cardboard box with his bayonet.

"Pall Malls for me," I said.

"Same."

He opened the box and tossed a carton to us. "That's all we got, you'll have to split it. Won't get any more for a week."

"Five's plenty."

"Not for me," Willy said. What else you got?

"All the menthols you can smoke. Everything else pretty much spoken for."

"Ugh. Gimme a couple packs of menthols, then. Just in case."

"Have a carton. You can always throw 'em away."

Willy and I helped Pop and the lieutenant stack sandbags around two sides of the hole. When Fats and Doc came back, all of us wrestled the six logs into place on top of the sandbags, then we went back to get the last two.

By the time we brought the two logs back, they'd covered half the bunker with three layers of sandbags. We placed the logs and finished piling up sandbags; wound up with four layers.

"Well, what do you think, Pop?"

"Four layers'll probably stop a sixty-millimeter mortar. Not much else. It'll do for tonight, though."

"Let's get some chow and call it a day."

"Goddamn it, Fats; get some chow, get some chow!—everybody else *hates* C-rations."

"Lieutenant Byrnes!" A private came running down the hill.

"Yes?"

"Command post wants you on the double!" He came to a staggering stop. "A Company's made contact, out in the boonies. Company-size ambush."

"Holy shit!" The lieutenant scrambled up the hill.

Pop grabbed the guy's arm. "Any casualties?"

"Yea. Don't know how many yet."

"Prof, better get ready to blow an LZ. Your demo bag up tight?"

He picked up a bag and rummaged through it. "Plenty of caps, fuse, det cord. We'll get a box of C-4 down at the pad."

Then the artillery roared, BLAM BLAM BLAMBLAM-BLAM; I jumped out of my skin and so did Willy, but the others didn't seem to notice.

"Farmer, Horowitz, go with the Professor. Wait on the pad 'til we send word."

We put on our packs, picked up rifles, and walked down to the pad. While we were on our way, three jets in tight formation streaked over the hill.

"That'll be air support," Prof said. "Watch."

Two of the jets peeled away and climbed, while the third went on for a half-mile, shot two rockets and a long burst of machine-gun fire, and climbed. A minute later the other two, about ten seconds apart, screamed over the hill again. The first dropped a load of bombs and the second dropped a large barrel that burst into an orange-and-black flower at tree-top level—napalm. They made a tight U-turn, rejoined the first jet, and sped for the horizon in tight formation.

"Whew! How do they know they aren't getting our boys?"

"Sometimes they do. Can't be helped."

Doc and the lieutenant came down the hill, carrying two chain saws and two axes. "Prof, you can scratch the C-4, they've got a natural LZ."

"Thank God for that."

"Yeah—look, the ambush dropped back after first contact, but they expect a night attack. They're digging in; you three got to go drop trees for their overhead."

"Coming back tonight?"

"No, you better count on staying. Doc's going along; they've got twenty casualties already. Sure to pick up more tonight.

"You new guys got plenty of ammo?"

"Two hundred rounds."

"Ammo dump's over there—better get another 500 apiece."

"Sir, our weapons aren't zeroed yet."

"Doesn't mean anything," the Prof said. "Never see your target out there anyhow."

"That's right. You get the first slick out—it's still a hot LZ, you'll probably have to jump."

I ran to get the ammo—I could hear the soft thrumming of a helicopter coming up the hill. Hot LZ? Jump?

How far did they expect us to jump without a parachute?

CHAPTER SIX

The slick brought us down, dropping like a rock, to within five feet of the clearing below. The copilot jerked his thumb and we jumped out.

Five feet isn't a long way to fall unless you happen to have a fifty-pound pack, a rifle strapped on your back, and a heavy chain saw in each hand. I hit hard, and fell over on my face. One chain saw ripped a chunk of skin out of my right leg. The chopper zoomed away, straight up.

"Hot LZ" means the pilot won't land, for fear of getting shot up. A couple of feet more couldn't have made that much difference, though. Besides, nobody was shooting anybody.

"Over here! Keep down!" A GI waved from the edge of the clearing.

The four of us got up and ran in a low crouch to where he was standing. "Are we glad to see you. You a medic?"

"Roger." Doc was staring straight ahead while he took the medic bag off his shoulder. I came up even with him and saw what he was looking at.

They had all the wounded and dead gathered in one place. The dead men, three of them were wrapped in ponchos. Blood had leaked out and settled in a pool under the three corpses.

Two of the wounded were sitting up, smoking; one with the side of his head all bandaged and the other with an arm in a makeshift sling. The other wounded were lying down, some of them unconscious. One man was naked from the waist down. Both his legs were blown off at the knee, stumps covered with scarlet bandages held in place by web-belt tourniquets. I heard Willy puke and clamped my jaws shut and swallowed hard again and again.

"God *damn* it, you didn't bring any blood?"

"Man," Doc drawled, "ain't *got* no fuckin' blood at the fire base. We come from Alamo."

"Sorry. We need it though, man, need it bad. Got any morphine?"

"Yeah, twelve syrettes, maybe fifteen."

"More'n all of us put together. Wanna go down the line and see if anybody needs another shot—but go easy, no tellin' what's gonna happen tonight."

"Ain't nothin' gonna happen tonight, man. The engineers is here. Charlie's scared of the engineers." He grinned and the grin was a skull's leer in a gray Halloween mask. I didn't know Negroes got pale.

"Let's go find some trees," Prof said, and clapped Willy on the shoulder. "Gonna be all right, Horowitz?"

Willy knocked his hand away. "I'll be OK." We went on into the woods.

About ten yards in, we hit the perimeter. Two guys were digging like mad while the third stood in front of them with an M-16. "Hands up, Prof," he said.

"Friendly, goddammit," Prof smiled. "Long time no see, Benson. Where's the captain?"

"That way." Benson gestured with his gun. "You gonna cut us some overhead?"

"Long as you keep Charlie away," Prof said.

"Hell, I thought you engineers was tough—chop 'em up with your chain saws."

"Must have been some other engineers you heard about. I'm chickenshit through and through." Prof didn't smile when he said that.

We walked on through the woods. "Last time I saw that guy I helped put him on a Medevac chopper with a bullet in his arm."

"They made him come back?"

"Yeah. Nice thing about the infantry, they don't let you get soft. Engineers who get wounded stay back in base camp the rest of their hitch."

"Glad to hear *that*."

"Mm-hmn. Best not to get wounded in the first place, though. There's the captain."

"You boys took your time." He was sitting by a radio with a map unfolded on his knees. He looked pale and his voice shook a little.

"Had to wait for a slick, sir, got here as . . ."

"OK, Prof, I know—drop your trees in the usual pattern, in a circle around the perimeter. Work fast, it'll be gettin' dark in a couple of hours."

"Yessir." We kept walking in the same direction. "Either of you know how to use a chain saw?" Prof asked. I didn't.

"Yeah, I worked on a farm one summer in high school," Willy said. "We cleared away some woods with 'em."

"Good. You know how to tell what direction it'll drop?"

"We always just made a notch on the side you wanted to fall, and then cut through from the back."

"Kee-rect. You take the yellow saw, the McCullough, and I'll take the green Remington; it's kinda cranky if you aren't used to it. Farmer, you'll be our security. Carry our guns and let us know if any shooting starts. We won't be able to hear a blessed thing once we start up the saws."

It was almost dark by the time we had dropped enough trees and cut them up into sections two ax handles long. While we were working two Medevac choppers landed—hot LZ or no—and took away the wounded men. Doc Jones left on the second one.

We didn't have time to dig a hole, but the artillery lieutenant said we could hop in his if caps started poppin'. We put our bedrolls under a tree by the artillery bunker and started to blow up our air mattresses. I was bushed, and I hadn't done much but stand around with three guns and a gas can, although they let me saw a couple of times to cut up logs.

"Now let me show you what every seasoned trooper

takes onto the battlefield," the Prof said, reaching into his pack. He pulled out three beers.

We drank the beer and tried to relax, but it was hard to keep calm and collected while the artillery bursts walked in a circle around our perimeter. That was supposed to keep Charlie away, and I guess it worked. I fell asleep about three o'clock in the morning, and there was no attack.

A godawful racket woke me just as the sun was coming up; birds and monkeys (and lizards, I later found out) screeching at each other. The Professor was already up, heating a can of C-rations the way he'd showed us yesterday.

"Morning, Farmer, drink coffee?"

"Yeah, sure." He tossed me three little brown paper envelopes. Instant coffee, sugar, and powdered milk.

"Use one of those beer cans for a cup, heat it up with some C-4." I had a steaming can of coffee in less than a minute.

"I forgot to bring any C's," I said. And I was hungry.

"They've got a couple of boxes down by the command bunker. But I wouldn't advise eating anything unless you're starving."

"I am, just about. Why not?"

"We're goin' on a burial detail this morning. Smell anything unusual?"

There was a faint sickly sweet smell, mixture of molasses and shit. "Dead people?"

"Dead and half rotten, in this heat. We've gotta put 'em under the ground, so don't eat anything if you don't have to."

"I thought they sent your . . . sent people's bodies back to the States."

"Sure, American bodies. Those are Vietnamese you smell. We search 'em, then bury 'em."

The coffee didn't taste so good. "Why do the engineers have to do it?"

"Sometimes the bodies are boobytrapped. Boobytraps're our job, not the infantry's."

"We gonna have to disarm boobytraps?"

"Nothing so fancy. We just blow 'em up from a distance."

"Sounds messy . . ."

"Yeah."

I poured my coffee out on the ground. It had too much cream anyhow.

"There's one over here. X-ray?" That was one of the infantrymen who came with us to help with the pick-and-shovel work, and provide security. They all called us X-ray, as if to remind us that we weren't heroic grunts like them.

"Okay," Prof said. "You two stay here for a minute. I'll check it out for boobytraps." He went into the woods where the guy had yelled, and came back a couple of minutes later, wiping his right hand on his fatigues.

"All set. Here." Prof handed each of us a cigar and lit one up himself.

"Thanks anyhow, Prof. I don't smoke the things."

"No time like the present to start, Horowitz. Keep it in your mouth and it cuts the smell." Willy lit up and so did I.

The body was lying on its back with arms and legs stretched out all the way. The Prof called it rigor mortis. The skin on his face and hands was black, blacker than a Negro's. His body was all puffed up to where it filled his uniform like a balloon. His mouth was stretched open wide, a swollen black sausage of a tongue forced between even yellow rows of teeth. His eyes were wide open and filled with ants. His body was covered with ants and flies.

"You guys are lucky. Don't have to start out with a bad one." Prof took a deep drag on his cigar and kneeled beside the body.

"Okay. This is how you check it out. First, make sure there aren't wires or strings attached to the body. Don't see any, do you?"

"Uh uh." I couldn't keep myself from looking at the eyes.

"Okay. Now you have to check underneath. They can

pull the pin on a grenade and prop it under the body, so it won't go off 'til you move it. Sometimes you can tell by just looking. Usually you gotta feel." He put his hand palm down on the ground and slid it under the body's back, sliding it back and forth. "Okay. He's clean. Now, Farmer, you do it."

"Aw, Prof, I get the idea . . ."

He stood up. "Still, you gotta do it."

I kneeled down where the Prof had and slid my hand under the corpse. Through the tight cloth of the uniform, I could feel the dead skin. Cold, spongy, slimy. I spit out the cigar and puked all over the dead man's chest. Prof put a hand under my arm and pulled me to my feet.

"Okay. It's a hard job, I know. Here, wash your mouth out." He handed me a canteen.

Horowitz kneeled down where the Prof and I had and repeated the action. Somehow, he didn't puke, though he looked a little green when he got up.

The infantry was digging a hole about ten feet away. "This deep enough, X-ray?"

Prof went over and checked it out. "It'll do. One of you guys want to give us a hand with the stiff?"

"Hell, no. We just dig the hole, man. That's *your* job."

Prof stomped back. "Horowitz, take one sleeve. I'll take the other. The grunts don't want to get their hands dirty."

"I'll help," I said.

"Don't have to if you don't feel up to it. Nothin' to be ashamed of."

"It's just a piece of meat. I don't mind." Like hell I didn't. But I know, if a horse throws you, you gotta get right back up on him. Or you'll never ride.

He was heavy. Horowitz took one sleeve and I took the other. Dragging him to the grave, my stomach tried to heave a couple of times, but it must have been empty.

We buried corpses all morning and through half the afternoon. After a while we saw what the Prof had meant, that we didn't "start out with a bad one." There were some bad ones, later on. Chunks of bodies we had to gather up onto a poncho and dump them into the hole. Man-shaped charcoal lumps, feather-light, burned crisp by napalm. And worse . . .

Finally we worked our way back around to the first grave and walked back up to the perimeter.

"Christ, Professor," Horowitz asked, "why don't we just move on, let them bury their own if they want to?"

"Usually, we do move on, never stay in one place longer than overnight. Took too many casualties, though. Have to stay here a couple of days, get replacements sent out."

"Still, why couldn't we just leave 'em—the smell's not that bad, back where we're camped out."

"It's a public health problem, Horowitz. The flies. If a fly lands on your C-rations . . . just remember where he's been."

"And open another can."

"Yeah."

CHAPTER SEVEN

We spent three days at the grave-surrounded "patrol base," with helicopters coming in almost hourly, bringing in new replacements, mail, and supplies from Alamo, and twenty-five cases of beer from God knows where. I managed to take it easy the last couple of days; once the base was dug in and the dead were buried, there wasn't much work for the engineers.

Our X-ray squad that had been with A Company all left that first day—one dead, two "lightly wounded." In fact, most of the casualties in the ambush had come from the center file, which was very unusual . . . normally, an ambush comes from one or both sides, and the flanks take most of the punishment.

So Willy and Prof and I were the engineer squad, and would be for at least a month. Prof assured us that it couldn't be as bad for us; engineers were the safest people in the whole company. But I couldn't help thinking that if Willy and I had come a few days earlier, it would've been *us* going out on that Medevac, wounded or dead.

A couple of days of sitting around, drinking beer, and reading (most of the guys were playing cards, but I only had ten dollars, which wouldn't last a minute) just about cured me of the shakes. The company set up ambushes all around the camp, but they didn't catch anybody, day or night.

We broke camp on the morning of the fourth day. Took

about an hour to fill the holes—emptied the sandbags, rolled 'em up, and tied them to our packs—and destroy all of the supplies we couldn't take with us.

We walked, and we walked, and we walked some more. Just like the Prof said, we walked in three lines; right flank, center file, left flank. I couldn't see the flanks very often, though, for all the jungle. Sometimes it was so thick—big trees, little trees, vines and underbrush—that the only guy I could see was Willy, walking in front of me. I hoped *some*body knew where we were going.

After a week or so it got to be routine. We'd walk all day and dig in a couple of hours before dark. The bunkers we dug each night weren't as fancy as the ones we had at the original patrol base—but we didn't have chain saws to cut overhead; a good man with a dull ax (they were all dull) takes ten minutes to cut down a small tree.

Then Thursday or Friday, I'm not sure which, the routine was over, all of a sudden.

The captain decided we'd stop on the side of a little hill that afternoon. The top of the hill was bald except for a half-dozen trees; we could cut them down for overhead and make an LZ at the same time.

Prof and Willy started digging the hole and I took the ax outside the perimeter, up the hill to cut down one of those little trees. I figured that one would give us just about enough overhead.

I took one whack and the forest below exploded in gunfire. I hit the dirt and crawled over to my rifle—I had propped it under another tree—jacked a round into the chamber and looked for something to shoot at. Couldn't see anything.

The shooting kept up, in short spurts, but it sounded like it was all on the other side of the company. At any rate, I couldn't see anything. I decided to crawl back down the hill.

The perimeter was about fifty feet away—think I set a new speed record for the low-crawl. All the men had dropped where they were working. They looked a little silly, trying to hide in holes no more than two inches deep.

Willy and Prof were in their little hole, Willy lying flat on his stomach, Prof on his back, smoking a cigarette and running a cleaning rod through his M-16.

"What's happening?" I flopped into the hole next to him.

"Cap'n sent out a couple of patrols, down the hill. One of 'em ran into some trouble. Don't know how many, yet." Another rattle of machine-gun fire, and Willy and I scrunched down into the dirt.

"Relax. They're still pretty far away. Probably don't know where we are, either."

The radioman came crawling over. "X-ray?"

"That's us," Prof said.

"Which of you was up on that hill?"

Oh, shit. "That was me."

"Come on, the captain wants to talk to you." We crawled to the captain, hiding behind some trees about ten feet away, talking on a radio.

"This the guy?"

"Yessir."

"X-ray, how many trees were up there?"

"Six or seven, sir."

"You've got to get them all down, right now. We've got at least two wounded, one dead—going to need a dustoff as soon as they can get back." I guessed that by "dustoff" he meant "Medevac."

"Find Sergeant Davis and have him detail you six men with axes. Run up there, chop 'em down, and run back. Better get a squad for security, too."

I went back to Prof. "Where's Sergeant Davis?"

"Left flank—guess he's out that way somewhere. Why?"

I told him what the captain said. "Well, Horowitz and I'll go, right?" Willy nodded. "Guess we need about ten more, with the security. Let's go."

Sergeant Davis was on the line closest to the shooting. "Can't give you no squad, man, I don't care *what* the captain said. If Charlie's comin' through, he's comin' through right here—I need every man I can get."

"Look, Sarge," Prof said. "They've already called for a

Medevac"—which was a lie—"and those wounded men might die if we don't get 'em right away."

"Bullshit. I've seen guys shot in the stomach hang around all day—'sides, if Charlie breaks through a weak line here, he'll wipe us all out."

"Okay, okay—give me two men with axes, I'll see how many I can get from the right flank."

"Simpson! Rodri-gez! Get axes and follow these X-rays." Simpson and Rodriguez scrambled over, looking relieved. Don't guess I'd care to stay on that line, either.

A buck-sergeant named Moselle was in charge of the right flank. *"Ten fuckin' guys?* Yer outa yer gourd, Professor. They's a war goin' on—can'tcha hear?"

"God damn it, Moselle. Nobody's firing on your flank. Anyhow, captain's orders "

"Awright, awright. B team! Up that hill—on the double!"

"Thanks, Moselle. Have 'em back in a couple of minutes."

"I'm comin' with ya to make sure."

"Bring an ax."

"Roger." He picked one up and the six of us ran up the hill in a low crouch. B team was already there, in a circle around a grove of trees. There were seven trees. We saved the smallest for last.

All but one of us dropped our trees, and Prof was working on the smallest one, when a grenade burst halfway down the hill, on the "enemy" side. We hit the dirt and rifle fire roared all around us, most of it from B team—maybe all of it.

"Get back!" Moselle shouted. "Back to the line!"

"Us, too," Prof said. "Go!" We ran like hell.

Prof went straight to his demo bag, started reeling out det cord.

"Can the dustoff land with those two trees there?" Willy asked him.

"Hell, no. Foul the blades. We gotta go blow 'em down." He cut off about eight feet of det cord and crimped blasting caps on each end. Then he snipped off about a foot of orange fuse and capped one end of it.

"Now, either of you ever blown a tree?"

"Not me," I said. Neither had Willy.

"Nothin' to it. One of 'em's cut halfway through, the other's little. A pound of C-4 each would knock 'em to Kingdom Come."

He got two bricks of C-4 out of his pack. "We'll use a pound-and-a-half each, just to be sure.

"You use the pointy end of the crimpers here, poke a hole in the C-4 to make a place to put the cap." He put a hole in one of the bricks, two holes in the other. His hands were shaking.

"Now get this. Don't have time to repeat it. Put one block at the base of the little tree, and one in the notch where Moselle was cutting the other. Connect the two with det cord, that'll make 'em go off at the same time. Then put the fuse in the other end of the block that has two holes. Light the fuse and *crawl* down the hill. Ninety-second fuse, plenty of time to crawl. If you get up and run, you might get shot."

"Which of us is gonna do it, Prof?"

"I am, of course—but if I don't make it, Horowitz tries, if you don't make it, Farmer tries. Farmer if *you* don't make it, some poor yoyo's gotta go up there with an ax."

I was a little disappointed that he put Willy ahead of me. Also a little relieved. We went back to the right flank.

"Moselle, I'm going up to blow those trees. Give me some cover, okay?"

"Sure. Jus' a second—Hey, Pig! Got that 60 set up?"

"Yeah, Moser—want I should shoot somebody?"

"Professor's goin' up the hill. Lay down a field of fire on his right."

The belt-fed machine gun chattered twice.

"Whenever you're ready, Prof. I'll get a couple of 16's to cover your left.

"Use my new men, Horowitz and Farmer."

"Okay."

Moselle put us in a "foxhole" (about a foot deep) on the

edge of the perimeter, facing the hill. "One of you guys start poppin' as soon as Pig starts the M-60. Bursts of three, about five seconds apart; aim anywhere to the Prof's left."

"That's this side?"

"Yeah, yer military left. Don't hit the Prof if you can help it. One reloads while the other fires—got it?"

"Sure, Moser." We set our ammunition in front of us. Together we had twelve magazines, clips with eighteen rounds each, plus 800 rounds in boxes. That was plenty, but refilling the magazines would slow us up.

It was my turn first. When the 60 started blasting—also short bursts, but about a second apart—I laid down a field of fire the way they taught us at Camp Enari. To get a burst of three you had to just touch the trigger, and get right off—if you held the trigger down any length of time, you'd empty the magazine, all eighteen rounds coming out right on top of each other. There wasn't any sense shooting close to Prof, there wouldn't be any enemy on the hillside. I sprayed the edge of the woods that started about fifty feet to Prof's left.

"Fer shitsake Farmer, don't shoot so fast! Five seconds!"

Guess I had fallen into the same rhythm the 60 was using. I sat down to reload and Willy got up to shoot. "Okay, Willy, I'll be more careful."

Pop-pop-pop. "You better. We might—" Pop-pop-pop. "—need this ammo more—" Pop-pop. "—after Prof gets back." Pop-pop-pop-pop. He was shooting just as fast as I had.

"Hey, Willy slow down yourself!" He started counting to five between bursts. Seemed like a good idea, so I did the same.

Seemed like it took Prof an age to get up the hill. But I was just starting my third turn when he got to the top, so I guess it was about two minutes.

In the movies, I guess Prof would get shot and Willy'd go up to rescue him, and Willy'd get shot and I'd go up and save the day, or maybe get shot, too . . . but actually, whoever had fired at us earlier was either gone or keeping his head down, because Prof set the charges, lit the fuse, and crawled back down the hill without drawing any enemy fire. When he got back to the perimeter he yelled "Fire in the hole!" three times, to warn everybody that the big boom wouldn't mean the Russians were coming.

It wasn't such a big boom anyhow—about as loud as one of the artillery shells we had gotten so used to hearing. The little tree flew away like a toothpick, and the bigger one gave a lurch and fell over. Lots of gray smoke and splinters flying.

The firing on the left flank had stopped before Prof went up the hill. When we went back, everyone was digging furiously, trying to build some kind of bunker while it was still light. Prof and I set to digging while Willy took the ax and got us some saplings for overhead.

It was almost dark by the time we finished. We were heating up some C's when we got word that we had to supply perimeter guards all night; two men on, one man off. That meant each of us would only get four hours of sleep. And boy, had I looked forward to hitting that sack.

Shouldn't have worried, though. Nobody was going to get very much sleep that night.

CHAPTER EIGHT

They attacked during the watch when the Professor was getting his four hours' sleep. Willy and I were on top of a bunker on the perimeter. It was about two o'clock and totally black.

We had orders not to shoot until we absolutely had to; the muzzle flash and tracer rounds would give our position away. We had plenty of hand grenades, though; and even though you can't see where you're throwing them, at least they can't be traced back to you.

There was a little radio in each foxhole, a PRC-25 (which everybody called a prick-25). Every perimeter bunker had a code name, starting with Tiger-1, then Tiger-2, Tiger-3, and so on up to Tiger-15. Tiger-1 was the command bunker, where the captain was. We were in Tiger-7. There were three observation posts, Oscar Poppa One, Two and Three; groups of four men each, sitting about fifty feet outside of the perimeter to give us early warning. Oscar Poppa Two was right out in front of us, and that was where the battle started. It started out real quietly.

The prick-25 whispered. "Tiger-1, this is Oscar Poppa Two. Over."

"Oscar Poppa Two, this is Tiger-1. Boss speaking." That was the captain's code name. "What's up? Over."

"We've got movement out front. Maybe fifteen meters. Over."

"How many? Over."

"Hard to say, Boss. More than ten. Over."

"Well, come back in. If they hear you, chuck some grenades at them. Out."

"Roger, Tiger-1. Oscar Poppa Two out."

"All stations, this is Tiger-1. Oscar Poppa One, Oscar Poppa Three, you come in, too. Tigers, hold your fire until all the Oscar Poppas are in. Over."

"Think we better go wake up Prof?"

"No," I said, "if anything happens, he'll be up soon enough—you scared as I am?"

"Shitless."

"Me too."

"Tiger-7, this is Tiger-1. Over."

Willy beat me to the radio. "Tiger-1, this is Tiger-7. Over." he whispered.

"Tiger-7, I want you to trade stations with Tiger-9; that's Pig's M-60 team. Over. Tiger-9, this is Tiger-1. Did you monitor that? Over."

The radio crackled. "Roger, Tiger-1, this is Tiger-9; we did monitor and we're on our way. Over."

"Well, at least we won't be so close if Charlie follows them in." I started gathering up grenades and ammo.

"Yeah, they'll walk right into that 60—think we oughta wait for Pig?"

"I guess so. Got everything of yours?"

"Six grenades, two bandoliers." Footsteps to our right. "That you, Pig?"

"Yeah. Y'all go on now, two bunkers over, leave your radio."

Took us about two minutes to find the place, even though we could see it before the sun went down. Pig's radio was squawking when we got there.

". . . repeat, all stations, everybody, in your bunkers. We have friendly artillery coming in on the old Oscar Poppa Two position. Over and out."

I jumped into the bunker and landed on top of Willy. He was pretty fast when he wanted to be.

"Jesus Christ—that's only fifty feet away!"

"We'll be all right in the—" the world bucked and heaved and shrapnel sang through the air. I could feel the artillery explosions in my teeth and my eyes. Willy's face was chalk-white in the light from the explosions. It only lasted a few seconds.

"Goddamn—you could see the flashes," Willy said. I could hardly hear him for the ringing in my ears. "They've never been that close before."

"Yeah . . . but think of what it's doing to Charlie."

"Let's hope."

After a minute a bunch of grenades went off, over by Tiger-7. Then automatic rifle fire, with green tracers, coming *into* camp. The artillery barrage hadn't gotten all of them.

Pig answered the rifle fire with his M-60, pouring lead into the jungle at ten rounds a second. Every third round was an orange tracer; it looked like he was spraying a solid line of flame.

A hand grenade went off pretty near, and in the flash Willy and I saw a man walking toward us, not more than ten feet away. I picked up my rifle.

"Wait!" Willy whispered. He pulled the pin out of a grenade and threw it side-arm out of the bunker. "Down!" I was already down.

It went off with a flat CHUNK and Willy got up and threw another. It went off and Willy said, "I think we better get out of the bunker."

"Are you crazy, Willy? With all that shit flying around?"

"Look, Farmer, all they gotta do is roll one grenade in here, and they'll be scrapin' both of us off the walls. Let's get out and lie down *behind* the bunker." I could see the sense in that, so we laid our weapons outside and hoisted ourselves up.

Looked like the battle was just about over. Pig's 60 was shooting in short bursts, but there wasn't any return fire. Tiger-6 and Tiger-8 fired M-16's into the jungle.

Then there was a whooshing sound and an orange ball of fire blossomed in front of Tiger-7. Somebody screamed. Another whoosh, this time the machine-gun bunker exploded and whoever was screaming, stopped.

"What the fuck is that?"

"Sounds like a bazooka," I said. "Does Charlie have bazookas?"

"Look, anything we've got, Charlie can steal. Just hope he doesn't have too many rounds."

"Think we oughta get back in the bunker?" Another whoosh. Hit just behind Tiger-6.

"Hell, no—you get in if you want. I'd rather take my chances up here."

The bazooka, or whatever it was, blasted a round right on top of Tiger-8. I was glad that we hadn't been shooting. He seemed to have zeroed in on everybody who'd given away their position with tracers.

Then we had a stroke of luck. The infantry had rigged the woods outside of the perimeter with trip flares, bright supersparklers that would go off if somebody tripped over a wire. There was a loud pop! and the jungle was flooded with light.

We saw them right away—two enemy soldiers in front of where Tiger-7 used to be, one of them with a long tube balanced on his shoulder. The other one had a bazooka round in his hand and another tucked under his arm. Willy and I opened up on them with our M-16's.

The ammunition bearer ran for the woods, and I think he got away. The other man was braver; he swung the tube around to where it was pointing at us, then one of us hit him and he flopped over backwards, shooting his last round into the trees where it exploded right over him.

That was the end of the battle. No telling how many enemy were involved, how many got away. We only found three bodies in the morning.

But the choppers took away three badly wounded GI's and six bodies, including Pig. That round, we had to admit, went to Charlie.

CHAPTER NINE

Willy and the Professor and I spent another three weeks in the field, without getting into any more fire-fights. Then one evening a chopper came in with three engineers, guys I'd never met (though they knew Prof), who took over. The three of us took the chopper back to the fire base.

The fire base wasn't on Alamo any more. They'd moved to a place called Plei Djaran, in the middle of a grassy field about a mile wide. They even had a landing strip for light planes. There was a mess tent serving two hot meals a day, and a beautiful river just down the road where we could swim a couple of times a week.

Nothing much happened the month we were there. We spent most of our time putting up barbed wire around the perimeter. At night we'd sit in the dark and drink beer when we had it, listening to Radio 560, the army's Pleiku station, which played mostly soul music, and a little country and western. One of the guys had some pot, but there wasn't any place we could go to smoke in privacy, and the Fourth Division is pretty strict about it; get caught and you'll spend a couple of months in LBJ, Long Binh Jail.

The three of us went back out to A Company on the first of May 1968. I was starting to feel like a real oldtimer, especially since most of the guys recognized me and Willy from last time. They had had it pretty easy while we were gone; only one light contact. The brass said things were quiet because the 66th NVA (North Vietnamese Army)

Regiment, who had been giving A Company such hell since February, had moved on south, toward Saigon. I didn't care what the reason was, but I was mighty glad that things were going to be less dangerous.

Sure enough, we moved around for a couple of weeks without so much as a peep from Charlie. Just walked around the boonies all day, dug in at night, got up in the morning, and humped all day again . . .

Things were going so easy that I guess I can't blame Prof for being careless. I might have done the same thing.

Prof and I were "walking point"; that is, we were at the front of the center file. I'd be in front for an hour, Prof second; then we'd switch and Prof'd be in front for an hour. This was the worst place to be in the center file, because you're usually the first one to go if you run into an ambush, and you get the first chance to step on any mines or boobytraps that might be along the path.

So when you walk point, you're supposed to be especially careful to watch the ground and not step on anything peculiar looking. Of course, you're supposed to watch the jungle, too, for whatever good it'll do. You can walk within five feet of a good ambush and not know it's there.

But the company hadn't ever come across a mine—they aren't common in the Highlands—and there hadn't been an ambush since the first day we joined the company.

We've got an antipersonnel mine, and I guess Charlie has it too, called a "Bouncing Betty." When a person steps on it, it doesn't just go off; first a little charge goes off that shoots it up to about chest-high, then it explodes.

I was looking off to the side when Prof stepped on the thing. It was pop-BANG! and I went down like I'd been hit by a truck. Pain like big bee stings up and down my left side. A big purple splotch was spreading along the inside of my leg. I clamped both hands over it and blood oozed out between my fingers. There was another stain welling out on my knee and while I watched I could see other, smaller ones, break out all over the leg. My left arm was covered with little bleeding pockmarks from tiny frags and blood started dripping from my chin. "Medic," I tried to shout, but it didn't come out too loud, so I tried again, and again, getting louder each time.

A medic came running up, crouched low. "Just lie down for a sec, Farmer, I've gotta check on the point man."

Prof was lying face-down in a puddle of blood. There was a hole in his neck so big that his head almost fell off when the medic turned him over. His face was blown away completely and his body was ripped open from throat to balls. I fainted.

I came to when they rolled me onto a stretcher. God, that hurt. My right arm was strapped to my side, blood feeding into it from a plastic bag a medic held over my head. There was a helicopter up the trail a ways, and they carried me there, walking very carefully. Guess somebody had told them to watch their step.

When they clamped the stretcher into the chopper, I saw that one of the guys carrying it was Willy. He grabbed my hand and said something, but I couldn't hear it over the roar of the slick's engine, so I just nodded.

It was a long ride. Seemed even longer when I saw what was on the floor, a rolled-up poncho with bloody boots sticking out from one end. Prof was going home early.

We landed in the Ban Me Thuot trains area, and two husky medics carried my stretcher down into a huge underground bunker, all lit up with fluorescent lights. They plonked me down on a table, and a man in a white coat came up with a clipboard.

"What's your name and serial number, son?"

"John Farmer, US 11 575 278." He wrote it down and put the clipboard away. He picked up a pair of scissors and started cutting away my trousers.

"Now we aren't gonna . . . take any stitches or anything, here—I just want to put new bandages on you and maybe give you a little shot. You'll be going to a regular hospital in about an hour." He also cut off my left boot. "Whoops—here's one the medic missed—son, did you know you'd been hit in the foot?"

"Can't say I did." It *did* hurt a little, now that he mentioned it.

"Well, it's just a little one. I'll fix it up." He took a big Band-Aid out of its paper covering and smoothed it over the wound. "Got your shot record in your wallet here?"

"I guess so."

"Mind if I dig through and find it?"

"Hell, no, go ahead." I wished he would just bandage me up and let me get some rest.

"Hmm . . . looks like I better give you a tetanus shot, just to be on the safe side." He produced a big wicked-looking needle and poked it in my arm. Funny thing, I hardly felt it. I asked him about that.

"Why, son, you're chock full of morphine . . . don't you remember the medic giving you a shot?"

"No, I was passed out most of the time."

"Oh. Well, that's why it dooon't hurt so bad. Let's take a look at these holes in you." He took the bandage off my head, and laughed.

"Just got a little scratch on your earlobe here, son; that always bleeds like a stuck pig. Doesn't mean anything, though; it'll be fine in a day or so."

He passed right over my arm and went to the large wound in my thigh. He started to untie the pressure bandage and some blood slopped out. "You're still leakin' a little bit here, partner—" He slapped a new pressure bandage on top of the old one and laced it tight "—but that one'll be okay, too, given time." The only other one that was still bleeding was the one on my knee; he put a new pressure bandage on it, too. The others he just wrapped up with gauze and tape. He wrapped a tube around my arm and took my blood pressure, and then pulled out the needle that was dripping blood into my other arm.

"You're in pretty good shape, son, all things considered." He took all the things out of my pockets and put them in a plastic bag. My wallet was covered with blood. He handed me the bag. "Now hang on to this until you get to the hospital in Tuy Hoa. They'll take it and lock it up for you, while you're in surgery."

"They gonna have to operate?"

"Sure, son, you don't want to go through life looking like

a piece of Swiss Cheese—and after they sew you up, you'll take it easy in bed for a few weeks. Just read funny books and goose the pretty nurses as they go by." He squeezed my shoulder and smiled. "You'll be all right, John." And I wondered if that was what Willy said when he put me on the slick.

"Chavez! McGill!"

"Yessir?"

"Take Mr. Farmer up to the waiting room and manifest him on the next flight to Tuy Hoa."

They took me to a large room with a bunch of empty stretchers and set me next to a table with a pile of *Reader's Digests.* I picked one up and leafed through it but had a hard time concentrating on the words. No need to give myself a headache on top of everything else. Besides, if I hit "Humor in Uniform," I'd probably puke.

With nothing else to do, I couldn't help but concentrate on the pain. It wasn't so bad, with the morphine, as I remembered it had been, first off; but it was still there—deep now, bone-deep and throbbing. "Medic?"

A guy came over, chewing gum, carrying the latest *Playboy.* "Yeah, champ?"

"You got anything for pain?"

"Just Darvon. Y'want a coupla Darvon?"

"If that's all you've got." He left for a minute and came back with two blue-and-gray capsules and a tiny cup of water.

"You don't wanna drink too much, now, not if yer goin' into surgery." He would say that. I was thirsty as a bitch.

By the clock, it was thirty-five minutes before Chavez and McGill came back to get me. They picked up the stretcher and one of them asked, "You ever ridden on an ambulance, fren'?"

"Never have." Ouch. My leg hurt every time either one of them took a step.

"Well, this will just be a short ride, but we'll put on the siren for you."

"Thanks a lot."

"Don' mention it."

They put me in the ambulance—it looked just like any other olive-drab army panel truck—and actually burned rubber on the dirt road, taking off. They switched on the siren. It might have been fun if I'd been in any condition to enjoy it.

There was a big bump—which hurt like hell—and we were on the airstrip, howling toward a C-130 that was all ready to go, engines roaring. They loaded me on and strapped my stretcher in place, and the plane was moving before the rear door had closed all the way.

I looked around. All the other people on the plane were sitting on the other side, perfectly well. There wasn't another wounded person on board—and for all the attention they paid to me, I could be just another piece of equipment. Thinking about it later, I guess that was all right. What did I want them to do? Stare?

CHAPTER TEN

The plane landed, not too gently, and there was an ambulance waiting for me. The ride in this one was just as fast and bumpy, but they didn't use the siren.

A couple of little Vietnamese unloaded my stretcher and jogged me down a covered sidewalk. The way they grunted and carried on, I was afraid they were going to drop me.

There was another building with bright fluorescent lights, this time aboveground. They put me on a table and a doctor came over (holding a clipboard, of course).

"John W. Farmer?"

"Yes, sir."

"Tell me in your own words what happened."

"We were walking down a trail . . . and the guy in front of me . . . stepped on a mine."

"How do you know it was a mine?"

"Well, it sounded like one, you know, a little . . . pop before it went off. A 'Bouncing Betty.' "

"Did it kill the man who stepped on it?"

All of a sudden I could see Prof lying on the trail with his guts rolling out, throat split open, after all the shit we went through together . . . and it could just as well have been me. I couldn't make myself answer.

"He *is* dead, then, right?" I nodded.

He asked me other questions about my unit, rank, and so on. While he was quizzing me an honest-to-God woman came over and cut away my dressings. She was about as old as my mother. Her touch was very gentle, but it still hurt when she peeled the dressings off.

She hooked my arm up to a bottle and said "Penicilin 10 million units USP"—I guess that was a supershot of penicillin. Must have been at least a quart.

Then one of the Vietnamese rolled me away, stretcher, table, bottle, and all. We went down the sidewalk about a block, and through double doors marked POSITIVELY NO ADMITTANCE. I wondered whether the Vietnamese could read English.

He rolled me up to a white table under a huge X-ray machine. A medic in a green tunic was talking on the phone.

"Right. He just got here. Okay . . . bye." He hung up.

"Well, Mr. John W. Farmer. Ready to get zapped by the Monster Machine?"

"Ready as ever, I guess."

"Hmm, that bottle's going to complicate things a bit." It was hanging on a rack attached to the rolling table. "We'll see what we can do, though." He motioned to the Vietnamese, and the two of them lifted me onto the cold enamel under the machine. "Now, we'll do the hard one first. Keep your arm stretched out so you don't pull the needle out, and roll over on your left side. Kick your good leg out to the left. Good. Hold it." He moved the machine around until the nose, a yellow plastic cone, was pointed at the biggest wound. It would have been an uncomfortable position even if I wasn't shot full of holes. He turned to the Vietnamese.

"Di di! Di di mao!"

I don't know much Vietnamese, but I know that *"di di"* means "get outa here" and *"di di moa"* means "get the *fuck* outa here." The boy left in a hurry.

"Now hold real still until I tell you. Good." He went off into another room and flicked a switch. The machine hummed for a few seconds. "Okay," he said, and came out of the room. Then he took pictures in two other, slightly more comfortable, positions.

He poked his head out the door and said something in Vietnamese I didn't understand. The boy came back in, they put me on the cart, and he wheeled me another couple of blocks.

We went into another building marked NO ADMITTANCE. It was air-conditioned, deliciously cool inside. We went down a hall and into a gray room. The only other patient was a Vietnamese with his arm in a bloody sling, screaming. A medic was sitting at a desk, ignoring him.

The boy wheeled me into position next to the screaming Vietnamese (who was a soldier, or at least wore battle fatigues). The medic filled a needle from a little bottle and came over to me. "You just get X-rayed?"

"Yeah."

"Well, this little shot'll make you feel better. You *are* John W. Farmer, aren't you?" He poked the needle into my arm.

"Right." Twenty Questions again.

"Yeah. Well, I'm gonna shave your leg, so the doc won't hafta look at all that hair." He soaped up an old shaving brush and lathered my leg. The Vietnamese soldier kept screaming.

"Look, shouldn't you be doin' something for that guy?"

"Nah. He's shot so fulla dope he can't be feelin' any pain. He's an enemy, though, NVA trooper they caught up by Kontum. Guess he thinks we're gonna torture 'im." Then I saw that he was strapped down, the buckles all out of his reach.

It's funny, I never could get up much hate for the enemy. Like I say, this is Johnson's fuckin' war, let him fight it. But I can't say I felt too bad about that guy, screaming bloody murder over a bullet in the arm. In fact, I'd rather have seen him lying on a jungle trail with his throat ripped out and giblets dribbling all over the ground. He couldn't have been the guy who buried the mine, not if they caught him in Kontum—but he'd do until the real thing came along.

The medic finished shaving me and I started to get a little woozy. Thought that shot was supposed to make me feel *better*. At least my ears were ringing so loud I could hardly hear the guy screaming, if he still was. For some reason, I couldn't focus on anything more than a few feet away.

The medic rolled me down to the other end of the room and through a door and into a room that seemed much darker and cooler. I remember an old guy with white hair and big bushy white eyebrows, wearing a green surgical mask, leaning over me, then everything shrunk away and I was out cold.

I woke up struggling against the straps that held me in bed, shouting and crying. A pretty little nurse held my hand and dabbed at my face with a piece of cotton.

"It's all over, soldier. You're gonna be just fine."

Nobody ever called me "soldier" before. But the way she said it, it was nice. She must have given me a shot—the world sprang into focus and I was wide awake. The first thing I saw was a big red NO SMOKING sign.

I looked up at her and asked, "Got a cigarette?"

"See what I can find." I watched her walk away. The white uniform was tight enough to give her a nice swivel. *That* was something I hadn't seen for a few months. Not that I'd stopped thinking about it.

She rummaged around in a desk drawer and came up with a stale pack of Kents. She brought them over with an ash tray and a pack of matches. First civilian matches I'd seen in a long time—they had a tomato sauce ad on the front and a recipe inside. I lit up, about the best cigarette I'd ever had.

She had gone back to her desk. "Say, is it all right if I undo these straps?"

"Sure. Just don't try to run around the block." She smiled. Jesus Christ.

I unbuckled the straps and looked under the sheet. All I was wearing was one big roll of bandage from ankle to crotch. There was a dark brown bloodstain on my thigh, over the largest wound. The whole thing ached, but I can't say that it bothered me too much.

"GI . . . ay, GI."

There was a Vietnamese strapped in the bed next to me.

I didn't recognize him at first, because he was wearing blue pajamas. Then I saw the cast on his arm and knew he must be the NVA who was carrying on so much earlier. He made smoking motions, quick little jerks with an imaginary cigarette.

I lit one up and passed it to him—not the easiest trick in the world, with both of us all tangled up in tubes and bottles.

"Cam on ong," he said. *"Toi la ban."*

I didn't catch most of that, but "come on" means thanks. Didn't know how to say "You're welcome" or anything, so I just nodded and leaned back in bed and smoked, watching the chick shuffle papers around her desk.

Whatever kept the leg from hurting wore off real fast. "Ma'am?"

"What would you like?" She smiled again. God damn.

"Can you give me something for the pain?"

She looked at her watch, and at a clipboard on the wall. "Not for another half-hour, I'm afraid. You could have a couple of Darvon, but I don't think they'd help much."

"Anything's better than nothing." Actually, I just wanted to see her walk again.

I took the Darvon and chain-smoked for a half hour. Then she came over again and gave me a shot. It stopped hurting before she even had the needle out, and I was asleep in a minute or two.

I dreamed that the NVA next to me was chasing me down a jungle trail, throwing lit cigarettes at me. My pack was full of blasting caps.

Somebody shook me awake; it turned out to be the medic who had shaved my leg earlier. "Wanna sleep yer life away, Farmer? It's breakfast time."

"Oh, man, go away." The leg was throbbing.

"Here, lemme crank you up." He turned a crank at the foot of the bed and the top half rose to put me halfway into a sitting position. "You'll feel better once y'get some chow inside."

The bed next to me was empty. "Where'd my buddy go?"

"Him? Oh, they took 'im to the POW ward last night. Here comes the chuck wagon."

A big Negro with a white uniform pushed a stainless-steel food cart down the aisle. "How 'bout some bacon an' eggs?"

"I have a choice?"

"Sure—you can have bacon an' eggs or a bottle o' sugar water, through another tube stuck in yer arm."

"Let me have the bacon without the eggs, then."

"Come on, man, just give 'em a try. You don't have to eat 'em." He filled a tray to the bed, loaded up a plate, and set it down in front of me, with a glass of orange juice and a glass of milk. "Want coffee?"

"Ugh."

"Suit y'self." He rolled the cart away, clattering like a junkyard on wheels.

Army scrambled eggs are enough to make a well man puke. I scraped them to the side of the plate and ate the bacon. The orange juice tasted like sour water, but the milk was good and cold. The medic saw I was finished and took away my tray.

I lit up a cigarette. "Got anything to read around here?" If the nurse had still been around, I would've been happy to just sit and look at her—but the medic was no prize.

"Coupla papers." He brought over a *Stars and Stripes* and an *Army Times*. I read every word in the first one, trying to get my mind off the leg, and got halfway through the second one. Then in came another medic, pushing a cart like the one I went to surgery on.

"John W. Farmer?" I don't know who else he thought it would be; there wasn't anybody else around but the other medic. I told him I was John W. Farmer, last time I looked. "Takin' you to Ward 8."

He wheeled me out of that nice air-conditioned room into a ward full of disgustingly well people. At least nobody else there had a tube stuck in his arm. Some of them were sitting on beds, playing cards. It was so hot I could hardly breathe.

I got a couple of Darvon from the nurse on duty, and

some writing paper and a pen. I tried to write letters to my folks and to Wendy, but the paper got so sweaty the pen wouldn't work half the time. I cussed and fumed, and the nurse gave me a couple of pencils.

Those were hard letters to write, trying to tell what happened without scaring the folks to death. So I lied a little bit here and there. I stuffed the letters into envelopes, addressed them, and wrote "free" up in the corner (that was the only advantage I'd found to being in Vietnam—didn't have to pay postage).

I slept until sundown and woke up with a start to the sound of a machine gun firing. There was a TV in the ward, and the patients were watching "Combat."

Half a dozen GI's had to take a farm building full of Germans, I mean really *full*, twenty or thirty of them, talking English with funny accents. Machine guns poking out of every window. Did they call in for artillery and wait? No— the ol' sarge in charge took a grenade and crawled across the open farmyard, bullets thick as flies, and tossed the grenade in through a window. Killed'em *all*. Guess they don't make grenades like they used to. Don't make bullet-proof GI's any more, either.

CHAPTER ELEVEN

I went to surgery again two days later (they had to wait until the smaller wounds were healing before they could close the big one), and stayed in Ward 8 until I could get around in a wheelchair. Then they moved me to another ward.

A week or so later, I graduated from the wheelchair to a pair of crutches. I still preferred the wheelchair, but with the crutches I could go across the sand to the PX, and out to the EM club at night for a few beers.

I pretty much settled into a routine. During the day I'd go down to the PX if I needed anything, then just lie in bed and read or write letters the rest of the day. Sometimes I'd wheel over to the next ward where they had a big percolator, and drink coffee. Every now and then I'd get into a checker game or play some whist. It was a pretty soft life, except for the ache in my leg. I'd ask for Darvon during the day and save it, taking them all at night when I got in from the club. Otherwise, I couldn't sleep.

Then one morning they took out my stitches. I had about a hundred of them, and some were covered up with scar tissue—my leg was a bleeding mess when they were through. The doctor said that all of the wounds had healed well, and I'd be leaving in a few days for the Convalescent Center in Cam Ranh Bay, for rest and physical therapy.

Turned out I had to leave the next day, along with a lot of others. The VC had attacked a bunch of people on their way to the voting booths in Tuy Hao, and the hospital was suddenly very overcrowded. Waiting for the bus that would take us to the airstrip, I saw helicopters unloading the casualties. Horrible—mostly women and children. There was a little baby crying with an eerie scream, high-pitched as a whistle; you could even hear it over the roar of the helicopter. When two medics ran by with the baby balanced in the middle of their stretcher, I saw that both his arms had been blown off at the shoulder.

As many dead people as I'd seen, as many wounded GI's and enemy soldiers . . . I'd rather bury a hundred rotting corpses than see that baby go by again.

The plan was an Air Vietnam DC-3, much nicer than the C-130's we usually rode on. I was the only person aboard with a crutch. (I could get along on only one by then, but there was one guy strapped to a stretcher, wearing a straitjacket. He spent the whole flight staring at the ceiling; he never moved once.)

We landed in about half an hour and took a bus to the sixth Convalescent Center. We filed into a big building where a sergeant took out medical records and gave us sheets and pillowcases. Ain't easy to walk with a crutch, carrying an armload of linen and a flight bag.

The bus waited while we were being processed and then took us to our billets. The driver called out names at each stop; I got off at the last one.

In front of the billet was an incredible beach—from horizon to horizon just as straight as if it had been laid down with a ruler. White sand and water so blue it was almost black. Two guys were riding surfboards in the breakers.

Inside the billet was like any army barracks, beds and lockers and not much else. I flopped my stuff down on the first bed I came to.

It's impossible to make a bed, standing on one leg with a crutch under your arm. I was just about to give up when a tall Negro came to my rescue.

"Heah, man, let me." It took him about twenty seconds to put the sheet on.

"Thanks—woulda been foolin' with that all night."

"Yeah. Say, you got a butt?"

I handed him one and lit one up myself. "What's it like around here? Beach sure looks nice."

"Shee-it. That all you gonna do, is look at it. Patients gotta get a pass to go swimmin'—but you don' get no fuckin' pass, 'cuz if you well enough to go swimmin', you well enough to go back to the boonies."

Sounded like I was back in the army.

"And that ain't the half of it, man—we got two mebee three formation a day, details all fuckin' day—PT in the mornin', man, gotta run a mile ev'ry mornin'—"

"No way nobody's gonna make me run. Can't half walk yet."

"Yeah, well, you safe long as you got that crutch. Fact, you just fall out in the mornin', push a broom around awhile. Then you free, rest o'the day."

Well, that didn't sound too bad. I found out that it was too late for chow, but there was an EM club that opened at seven. I hobbled over there and waited for it to open.

I managed to fill up on Slim Jims and beer. Watched TV until the place closed at eleven.

Army television in Vietnam is pretty strange. They show reruns of Stateside shows, usually a year or so old. And the commercials are made by the army—telling you to keep your weapon clean, buy bonds, don't inflate the Vietnamese economy, and so on.

Seemed like I just barely got to sleep when they rousted us out of bed. My watch said quarter to six. It was still dark. I got my shaving kit and hobbled out to the shower.

It was almost worth getting up that early, though, because they had hot water. It was quite an experience, after shaving with cold water for four months. And the shower was pure heaven, even though I had to leave my crutch and hop across the slippery floor like some weird kind of bird.

The guy in the shower next to me looked at my leg. "Man, you really got fucked-up good."

"Yeah. Land mine."

"No kiddin'—you must be the only wounded guy in this barracks. Most everybody else's here for the clap or malaria."

"What about the other guys on crutches—some case of clap they must of picked up."

"Nah—broken legs. No other heroes."

Hero, that was a laugh.

We had a formation at six-thirty, everybody standing around in their blue pajamas while the first sergeant read off a bunch of announcements. I heard that I was supposed to report to room 101 at 1330 for physical therapy. After he finished the announcements he said. "Cripples, fall out and get yer brooms," and everybody who had a crutch or a cane went back into the barracks. It took us about five minutes to clean it up. Then some of the guys went to chow. I was so tired I just racked out for a few hours.

It was hotter'n hell when I woke up, about ten o'clock. There wasn't anybody else in the billet. I figured they must've gone someplace where it was cool, so I gathered up my crutch and set out to find them.

Went about a block down the main drag when I heard these monster air conditioners chuggin' away. It was the library. Sure enough, it was crowded—there were only three seats left. I found a bunch of books of cartoons and sat in the cool until noon, just diggin' it.

There was a formation at 1300, but we cripples didn't have to go to it. So I put off chow until about 1230, then walked over to the mess hall.

It was hot as a steam room in the mess hall. Can't complain too much, though. Since I had a crutch, I didn't have to stand in line; I just sat down and a Vietnamese girl brought me a tray full of food. Not bad, either, by army standards; two hamburgers, french fries, and a salad.

After chow I wandered over to 101, the physical therapy

building. It was air-conditioned there, too—but pure torture. I spent an hour lifting weights (little sandbags) with my bad leg, hurt like the very devil. They gave me a Darvon for my trouble and I limped back over to the library.

I felt better after sitting in the cool for a while, so I decided to go out and explore some. Would be a great place if you had any money to spend—snack bar (with pizza), big PX and a gift shop—but I only had eleven dollars, and I decided to save it for beer. That would be 110 beers, a couple weeks' worth.

I wound up in a big recreation hall run by the Red Cross. They had all kinds of games and stuff. Played a few games of checkers with a Red Cross guy named Jerry. He beat me every time, but in return he told me how I could get some money—there was a man from the Fourth Division who could get me up to twenty bucks a week, that'd be taken out of my pay later. I decided I could afford a pizza tomorrow.

There was another formation about sundown, but all that happened was that the First Sergeant called out the names of the guys who'd be leaving in the morning. Then he let us go to chow (which was pretty fair beef stew).

For a couple of weeks I did pretty much the same thing every day. Kind of made the rounds between the library, the Red Cross center, physical therapy, chow, and the EM club. Sometimes I'd hang around the PX and read the magazines. Not real exciting, but sure beat the hell out of being a combat engineer.

Then my leg got better and they took away my crutch. That made all the difference in the world. The next morning I couldn't fall out after the first formation, and I had to take PT.

The first exercise was jumping jacks, you know, where you jump up and down and swing your arms around—like a guy who's on fire and trying to put himself out. No way in hell I was gonna try one of those.

The guy who was leading them glared at me all through the exercise and, when they were finished, yelled out:

"Whatsamatter, soldier, you on vacation?"

"Have a heart, Sarge, I just started walking yesterday."

"So you don't think you can do jumping jacks."

"That's right, Sarge."

"What *can* you do?"

"Dunno, Sarge."

"Try twenty pushups. Righ now."

That shouldn't have been hard; I was doing eighty every day in Basic Training—but I could only do twelve, and had to fake the rest of them, with everybody watching. A month in the hospital can really put you out of shape.

Had to fake most of the other exercises, too, except for the arm twists. And when they got out on the road to run their mile, I just limped along behind at a slow walk. A different guy was leading the running, and when he saw me lagging behind, he dropped back.

"Somethin' wrong with yer foot, fella?"

"Just got off a cane yesterday."

"Well, fall out and go to chow. Don't sweat the run."

First nice thing anybody had done for me in some time.

The work formation was right after chow. I got assigned to sandbag detail, one of those jobs that never ends. Since we had more empty sandbags than we could fill in a week, we just took is as slow and easy as we could.

At 1300 I went to my physical therapy appointment. Didn't even think about the 1330 formation. But, since I wasn't a "cripple" anymore, I was supposed to be there. And people who skip the midday formation get put on the next day's shipping roster.

I didn't find out until the next morning, when the First Sergeant called out the names of the people who were leaving. Instead of going to PT, I limped into the orderly room. The only guy there was a private, reading a comic book, feet stuck up on a desk.

"Hey, man."

"Yeah?"

"Can you tell me what the fuck I'm doin' on the shipping roster today?"

"Whatcher name?" I told him. He looked at a clipboard, hanging by the desk.

"Says here, 'AWOL 1330 formation.' Musta been yesterday—what, didya skip out?"

"No, man, I couldn't make the fuckin' formation; I had a physical therapy appointment."

"Shoulda told somebody. Right now, you better find some doctor who'll give ya an excuse in writing. Otherwise you gotta leave at nine o'clock."

I went down to the infirmary. There was a fat sergeant at the admissions desk.

"Sarge, I gotta see a doctor."

"Your name on sick call?"

"No, it's not."

"Well, you better get on sick call or you won't see no doctor."

"But Sarge, it's after seven. I can't get on sick call this late."

He shrugged. "So don't die here. Go find a medic at the emergency room."

"Sorry, Sarge, a medic won't do."

"Oh, you gotta have brain surgery or somethin'. What's the score?"

"Well, they put me on the shipping roster today—"

"Congratulations."

"Goddammit, Sarge, I can't half *walk* yet!"

"Look, son, I get twenny guys come in here ev'ry morning tryin' to get off the shippin' roster. Tough shit, all of 'em. I ain't never let one through, never will."

"Sarge . . ."

"Yer all just a buncha chickenshits, don't wanna go back an' fight." He was shouting, and I could smell whiskey. "I was in Korea . . ."

"Bet you were tough, Sarge." I'd rather have killed that

motherfucker than all the VC in the world. I slammed the door good and hard on the way out.

So at nine o'clock I rode a bus to the airport and got on a C-130 to Pleiku.

CHAPTER TWELVE

I walked in through the captain's door and came to attention in front of his desk. "Private Farmer reporting for duty sir."

"At ease, Farmer. Have a seat." I sat down across from him.

"For one thing, you aren't a PFC anymore. Your orders for Spec/4 came in right after you were wounded."

"That's good news."

"Yes, and the army owes you some money. You can go down to Finance and get it, any time you want.

"Now, Farmer, you probably know I don't order men back into the field, once they've been seriously wounded. I've kept a job open here at base camp, assistant to the supply clerk. Don't suppose you want it."

"Sure do, sir."

He chuckled. "Can't say I blame you. He'll run you ragged, though . . . you were limping when you came in. Wounds still bother you?"

"Yes, sir. I had to leave the hospital before I was finished with physical therapy." I told him the story about the formation I missed, and how I got railroaded out.

"That's unfortunate, but I suppose it happens all the time. Tell you what, after you go to Finance, drop by the battalion aid station and see whether they have any physical therapy equipment. At least they should be able to set up some exercises for you to do.

"I'll put you on light duty status"—he pulled out a pad and scribbled something on it—"and you can do your physical therapy instead of coming to the morning formation." He handed me the paper. "This is good for three weeks. If anybody asks you to lift something heavy or walk any great distance, just tell them you can't. They can check with me."

"Thank you, sir." The slip said "Sp/4 J. W. Farmer, light duty to 30 June."

My back pay, with the promotion, came to almost 500 bucks. I pocketed fifty and put the rest in the company safe. It turned out they didn't have any physical therapy equipment at the battalion aid station, but the doctor there had a book that showed three exercises I was supposed to do for the leg. They weren't as bad as the sandbag-lifts at Cam Ranh Bay, but they did hurt some. Still, got me out of morning formation.

My new job, helping the supply clerk, was dull as hell. Most of the time I just cleaned equipment that wasn't really very dirty. Sometimes I'd make lists, type 'em up, and file 'em away where nobody would ever see them.

One day I was cleaning up, getting ready to close the supply room for the night, when the door opened—and a hand grenade flew in!

I started to roll under the counter when I saw it was harmless, the arming lever taped down securely.

"Awright, who's the wise fucker?"

"I cannot tell a lie. I am the wisest fucker in the company."

'Willy!'

He was just as mangy-looking as ever—conditions in the field hadn't improved any—so I got him a new set of fatigues and a bar of soap. After he cleaned up and changed, we went over to the EM club.

"Well, Farmer, how do ya like bein' a base-camp commando?"

"Beats the hell outa humpin'."

"Hmm—I don't know. It's been pretty easy since you

left. With the monsoon coming up, we aren't humping as much. Mostly just stay in fire bases."

"And you don't have to shine boots or salute officers."

"That's right. I understand old General Stoner's a real sonofabitch for military courtesy."

"Yeah—shit, it's gettin' to be just like Stateside. Inspections every morning. If it moves, salute it. Have to go through the fuckin' chain of command to talk to anybody. What a bunch of bullshit."

"So why don't you volunteer for field duty again, man? We've got it easy."

I *had* thought of it, but . . . "No way, Willy, I can put up with anything for another four months. Just wanta get out of here alive."

"Yeah, I was just kidding, I guess. Half kidding, anyhow. Showers every day and cold beer every night—fuck, you've got it made."

We talked for a long time, mostly about what we were going to do when we got back to the world. Just about talked each other into going back to school. Couldn't hurt.

Willy was dead tired, so we left before the club closed. The next morning I drove him down to the pad and put him on a bird to the fire base. He still looked pretty shot. I was doubly glad to be where I was.

Base camp life went along as usual for me, pretty dull and a little bitchy. Then one day I was walking along the road, coming back from the PX, when a jeep passed me, stopped and hauled-ass in reverse back to me. There was a little flag with one star, fluttering on the bumper. I dropped my package and came to attention. General Stoner.

The driver, a captain, got out of the jeep and walked up to me. "Soldier, you are in trouble."

"Yes, sir."

"The General feels that, if a person can't be bothered with military courtesy in base camp, not even to the extent of saluting a general . . . he should be sent someplace where he won't have to worry about military courtesy."

General Stoner was sitting in the back seat, staring straight ahead, not looking at me. I'd heard of this; don't salute Stoner's jeep and zap, you're out in the boonies. Never thought it'd happen to me, though. Hell, I'd never even *seen* his jeep before.

The captain whipped out a leather-covered notebook. "What's your unit—who's your commanding officer?"

I told him and he wrote it down. Then he got my name and serial number (and checked my dogtags to make sure I wasn't lying.)

"Report yourself immediately to your company commander and tell him what happened. Tell him you request immediate transfer to a field position."

Yessirs and salutes and all that bullshit, and he got back in the jeep and drove off. I went back to the company and reported to the captain.

"Jesus Christ, Farmer, you really blew it this time, didn't you?"

"Yes sir, I did."

"Well, I'll send you out to the fire base where your old platoon is. They haven't had any action for over a month, so it shouldn't be too bad. But I don't know how soon we can bring you back . . . how short are you?"

"Three months, sir."

"Hmm—we'll try to get you back in base camp your last six weeks.

"Well, go get some field gear and run down to the pad before it gets dark. Better hope you can get a ride out, too. We'll both be in hot water if you're still here tomorrow."

So I requisitioned myself a pack and a gun, canteens, and grenades (you can carry them on choppers) and all that junk. It took me a half-hour's wait to get a slick, and another half-hour to get to 2124, which the pad man told me was about thirty clicks—kilometers—west of Pleiku. That's about eighteen miles.

The fire base had moved to an old abandoned tea plantation. They were serving chow out of a falling-down farm building (still, better than C-rations), and the medics were set up in an old barn—just sitting around playing cards, which was a *very* good sign. There was even a dirt road leading into the place.

I found the engineers, but Willy wasn't there—in fact, the only guy I knew was Doc Jones, the engineer medic.

"What you doin' back here, man? Thought you was in some soft base camp job."

"If I told you, Doc, you wouldn't believe me. Where's Horowitz?"

"Out with D Company. S'posed to come in tomorrow."

"Thought they weren't humpin' any more."

"Jes' overnight stuff, ambushes." Doc introduced me around to the new guys. Sergeant Miller, the new platoon sergeant, put me to work cleaning chain saws. Said he wished he had something better for me to do, but it was either that or fill sandbags.

The last chopper in was a big Chinook, or "hook," a boxcar-sized chopper with a monster load of beer and soft drinks. The engineers got six cases of beer and two of soft drinks. After we split them up and traded around (two beers for a soda), I wound up with twenty-one beers (and no sodas, never learned to like them warm).

We decided to do some serious drinking that night. Sergeant Miller produced a fifth of Scotch—God knows where he got it—and we sat in a circle, passing the Scotch around, washing it down with beer, tellin' lies.

Most of my memory of that night is pretty fuzzy, both because of all the drinking and because of what happened the next day. One thing I *do* remember, though, was when Doc Jones lit into me.

He was telling a joke about two Negroes on a motorcycle having a run-in with a white cop, and when he imitated the cop talking, he sounded like any regular white man, no black accent at all. I thought we were good enough friends, so I asked him straight out why, if he could talk regular English, he didn't talk that way all the time.

It must have been a sore spot, or maybe I was just stupid to ask in the first place—I didn't have any Negro school-mates in Enid and was just curious—but he really blew up. Where had I been all my life, he asked, that I thought there was only one way to talk English—people talk the way it's most comfortable, the way they're brought up. Besides, he said, I sounded like Chester on *Gunsmoke*; half the time *he* couldn't understand a word *I* said! Everybody took Doc's side, and I felt like a real hick. Things got back to normal before we'd finished the bottle, though.

As the old saying goes, "beer on whiskey, mighty risky." I got to feeling woozy after a couple of hours, and went off to hit the sack. I remember starting to blow up my air mattress, but when I woke up in the morning I was lying on the cold ground, the air mattress on top of me without any air in it. Maybe that was because I forgot to put the plug in when I finished blowing it up.

"Wake up, Farmer. Just got time to say goodbye." Someone shoved a can of steaming black coffee under my nose. My head throbbed with every heartbeat.

"Willy—thanks. What time's it?"

"Little after seven. Everybody else is asleep down in the bunker. You decide to live dangerously? or just hanker to sleep under the stars?"

"Musta passed out. Little party last night—you got an aspirin?"

"No, but I can probably find Doc's bag." He started rummaging around the pile of rucksacks and stuff alongside the bunker. "All that time I was lying out there in that ambush, trying to stay awake, you guys were lappin' it up—here we go." He brought over a couple of white tablets and a canteen.

"Thanks. Anything happen on the ambush?"

"The usual. One guy fell asleep and got chewed out. Otherwise, no excitement." He took a loud slurp of coffee. "Now, what the hell are *you* doing out here?"

"Oh, man, don't ask. It's so stupid."

"Didn't volunteer, did you?"

"Fuck, no! It was . . . well, General Stoner's jeep drove by me . . ."

"And you didn't salute?"

"Yep. So here I am."

"God damn—it's true, then. Always thought that was just a bullshit line they made up to keep you saluting."

"No way. I'm out here for six weeks at least."

"Probably won't be in the fire base much, either."

"Huh?"

"Fact—Miller'll probably have you take over my job, field squad leader. Nobody else here has more than a month's experience, except Doc. And he's not an engineer, not by training."

"Shit . . . trouble just comes in bunches, doesn't it." And the aspirin wasn't helping my head.

"Don't sweat it, man. We stay in fire base a couple of days every week. And in the field, well, we've only had one shootemup since June. Charlies' gone from around here."

"Let's hope. How much longer you stayin'?"

"Be on the first bird to base camp."

"That soon!"

"Yeah, man, I'm really short. Eight days. I'll be home before the next time you shave."

"Oh, you dirty fucker. And me with ninety days . . ."

"Right, John—next time you pick up that razor, think of me back home in Manhattan, in school, good threads and a pretty chick on each arm—wait!" Sound of a helicopter, pretty far off. "Think I hear the subway comin' in. Want to walk over with me?"

I was still trying to imagine what Willy would look like with clean clothes, civvies at that, and no whiskers on his chin. Just couldn't see it—let alone the two girls! "What?"

"Want to walk with me down to the pad?"

"Sure. Maybe I can knock you over the head and steal your papers."

"No way you'd ever pass for me, Farmer. You're too pretty."

What do you say to a guy who's going back to the world? We just stood on the pad, Willy watching the slick get closer and closer, me feeling a little bit jealous and sorry for myself.

Just before the chopper landed, Willy shook hands with

me and wished me good luck. I wished him the same, though he was just about past the need for it.

The noise of the bird hadn't helped my head any, and it woke up the sleeping drunks in the bunker.

Drinking his morning coffee, Sergeant Miller said yes, I'd be doing Prof's job, at least until White, the assistant squad leader, had learned enough to take over.

He said we'd be humping out early in the afternoon, to set up a company-sized night ambush about two clicks away.

Turned out we left at noon.

CHAPTER THIRTEEN

Started out easy enough. We humped for about three hours and then set up a box-shaped ambush around a place where two jungle trails came together. We napped in shifts until dark, since Charlie doesn't travel much during the day. From sundown to sunup, though, we all had to be on alert.

This company had been setting ambushes for over a month without a single night of action, so nobody was surprised when the sun finally came up without a shot being fired. Tired as I was, I might as well have spent the whole night doing pushups.

The captain decided the hell with it, we'd hump back to fire base and get a day's rest. We could've stayed at the ambush place for another night, but I guess he didn't think it'd be worth it.

Maybe the captain should've let us rest before we started out. But everybody was anxious to get back to the fire base, get a hot meal, and sack out. So tired, careless, we started to hump back.

After about an hour, the jungle got less dense and the path we were following widened into a small clearing. I remember thinking it was strange to be able to see both flanks and the center file all at once, but it didn't occur to me that that was extremely dangerous.

Then one of the flankers yelled and fired. I hit the dirt

and jacked a round into the chamber of my M-16 and all hell broke loose.

Ambush on three of four sides, just like we had sat in all night; a classic box. The gunfire mounted in a steady crescendo until it was just one constant unnerving roar. They had fifties, three fifty-caliber machine guns that traversed back and forth over the little clearing; perfect setup for a hundred careless idiots. A fifty is a hell of a lot of gun—all we had to fight back with was regular humping-infantry stuff; M-16's and grenades and one M-60 without too much ammo. You could barely hear our return fire over the chug of those fifties.

A minute ago I could see almost all of the company, seventy or eighty men. Now, lying in the grass, I could only see three, and one of them was dead.

The radio operator and White, my assistant squad leader, were lying in front of me. A rifleman whose name I'd forgotten, one of the flankers, was in the elephant grass to my left, his ribs glistening white and splintered where a rifle grenade had dug out his chest.

After a minute the enemy slacked off; fire started coming in short bursts. The radioman was hollering into the horn, trying to get us some artillery. The artillery observer, Lieutenant Hernandez, was thrashing around in the grass with a sucking chest wound, not interested in giving coordinates to the radioman. Finally, a shell crashed into the jungle, but it must have been a mile away.

The captain crawled up to me, moving on his back like a swimmer trying to do a backstroke with his shoulders.

"Where the fuck is that medic?" He had his left hand cradled in his right, blood gushing from the stump of a thumb.

"I don't know, Cap'n, he was back of me somewhere." The captain started to worm his way back. "Hold up—you stay here, I'll go back and find him. Got to check on my squad anyhow."

He opened his mouth to say something, then shut it and nodded. Not that I was bucking for a Bronze Star. They

don't make engineer heroes. But I had to get my men together.

Squirmed out of my pack and demo bag and started
crawling, rifle slung between my arms like some basic
trainee on the "live fire" course. This was live fire, all
right—but the bullets came in a little lower here.

"Medic!" I shouted once and rolled away, knowing they
might zero in on the noise.

"Over here, goddammit," came a whisper to the left. It
was Doc Dayton, the center-file medic. I found him in a
shallow depression behind a stand of saplings, bandaging
a tall Negro flanker whose lower jaw was shot off, thick
blood drooling around the pressure bandage.

"Where you hit?"

"Not me, Doc—the captain's bleeding pretty bad from a
hand wound and Lieutenant Hernandez got shot in the
chest—"

"Motherfucker musta stood up."

"They're both up front. Ten meters or so."

A burst of machine-gun fire rattled through the saplings. The medic and I cringed down, but the big Negro just
lay there, eyes filming. "Fuck 'em both." Doc pushed a
morphine syrette through the dying man's sleeve, blood-
slick and shiny. He tagged the man's collar and said,
"Let's go."

"Gotta check my squad first."

"Man, you ain't *got* no fuckin' squad—go back there and
you won't have no fuckin' squad leader, neither."

"All dead?"

"Dead, wounded—fuckin' half the company blown away
'fore they could hit the dirt."

The captain was lying beside the radioman when we
crawled up. "Drop on-zero-zero and fire for effect. One-two
over and out." He hung up the horn and saw us behind
him. "Doc, go check the lieutenant, I think he's dead. Find
your squad, Farmer?"

"Doc says they're all gone, all but me and White."

"Not White." The captain glanced at my assistant

squad leader's body, less then five meters away, the back of his helmet blown open and bluish-grey brains splashed in a bloody streak down his back. "You'll have to drop back and try to blow the LZ by yourself."

"No way, Cap'n. That's suicide—I need a squad of riflemen with me while I set the charges, or—"

"That's an order, Farmer. Sorry. We need every man we can get on the line." He drew in breath with a hiss when Doc clamped a tight bandage over his hand. "Where the fuck is that artillery?" We all looked up automatically at the faint tearing sound that came in answer. "Get down that's coming right on top of—"

Everybody was already down, of course, but I held my helmet on with both hands and pushed my face into the dirt.

The ground fell away and came back to slap me, twice, three times and my ears rang, chimes, buzzers, bells . . . the captain shouting came through a whisper.

"Sergeant, round up a squad and try to punch through in the front. You go with them, Doc; see if you can find a place to blow your LZ."

It was useless to argue, and I supposed going up front with a bunch of riflemen was better than trying to get through the rear by myself. I picked up my demolition bag, put a couple of grenades on each side of my belt, and set out, ax in one hand and M-16 in the other.

We couldn't find a squad of whole people, but we got ten grunts and a medic, plus me and the sergeant. The fifty that had been spraying right down our column hadn't fired a shot since the artillery salvo hit. But they could just be playing possum. We circled around the gun's position and closed in.

I was crawling up the center between the medic and the sergeant when an AK-47 opened up on the right, a sound like dry sticks cracking. A couple of grenades went off and the AK stopped. That was all the resistance we hit.

One of the eight-inch shells had come in right on the fifty; nothing but twisted metal and gallons of blood scattered all over the area, with some barely recognizable human parts. Crawling up, I squashed an eyeball with my elbow.

There were a dozen or so shattered bodies just beyond where the salvo had hit. No telling how many had slipped away.

"Wanna blow your LZ here?"

I looked around. "No, it's too close to the perimeter. Those trees're too big anyhow. I don't have enough C-4 to drop all of 'em."

"Well, I can't send my boys out too far. They're still fightin' back there, back at the rear." I could hear spurts from the fifty that must have taken out my squad. "Might have to go back any minute."

"I know, goddammit." I could see daylight ahead about forty or fifty feet. The trees were probably more sparse there. "Leave me five men and take the rest back to the captain."

"Who's given' orders here? I'll let you have three."

"Whatever you can spare, Sarge. But you know there's nothing more important than that LZ now—we're gonna need ammo, and we got thirty or forty wounded; a lot of 'em are gonna die if they don't get a dustoff, quick."

"All right, take the fuckin' five—but make it quick! I'm gonna need everyone of 'em on the line."

We got to the sunlit area with no trouble, six of us moving up in a zigzag line. "Skinny, take three guys and post guards out, oh, thirty feet. Leave me Tex to help chop down that bamboo."

"How long a fuse you puttin' on it?"

"One minute—when I holler 'fire in the hole' you got a little less than that to take cover. Or you can head back to the perimeter; that's what I'm doin'."

"Minute's not too fuckin' much time."

"Nobody's gonna get blown away, Skinny—I don't have that much C-4. Just get far enough away that a tree won't fall on you."

"OK, Farmer—Tex, get to work on that bamboo. Rest o'you poor fuckers follow me."

Tex had just about gotten the bamboo down by the time I had set the first charge. It was a big one, ten pounds of C-4 set into a hole I chopped out of the base of a tree. I was crimping a cap when the sergeant came back.

"I need those five men. Need 'em *bad!*" He was panting hard. "Gooks broke through our rear, we're split in two."

"Well, they went that way. Leave me Tex, OK?"

"No way. Need all the firepower we can get—you're goin' on the line yerself, soon as you blow those trees."

Decided I'd take my time on the trees. I'm nobody's infantryman. Of course, I wasn't too happy about being left alone in the woods, either. The fighting was quite a ways away, but the enemy might decide to circle around, and run into me. In fact, they probably *would* circle around and try to surround us.

The sergeant took his men back and I continued setting charges, working as quietly as possible.

I was almost through, molding the last of my C-4 into the crotch of a tree that poked out of the ground like a giant wishbone, when I heard somebody coming down the path, from the wrong side. I got down behind a bush.

A Vietnamese wearing green jungle fatigues—probably an NVA regular, no VC would look that military—walked into the semi-clearing where I had set my explosives. He was carrying an AK-47 but also wore a pistol; probably an officer. I eased the safety off my M-16 and worked a hand grenade from my belt. Then I realized I couldn't use the grenade without setting off the whole thing—no matter what I told Skinny, it wouldn't be healthy to be near it when it went bang. I just wanted to kill the guy, I didn't want to share a grave with him.

Each charge was connected to two others with a length of white det cord, to make sure they'd all go off at once. The officer didn't see it at first, and just kept walking down the path. He'd pass about five feet in front of me.

Then he saw the stuff, turned and said something in a

soft voice to the woods behind him. Four more men came out, following down the path. They knew what it was and wanted to get away.

I drew a bead on the officer, who looked like he was waiting for his men to catch up with him, and squeezed off a burst. Popped holes in his hip and back, and he flopped to the ground jerking. The others took cover but didn't shoot.

At first I didn't think they knew where I was hiding, so I held my fire, hoping they'd retreat. Then I heard the clink! sound of a grenade, the arming lever springing off as one of them threw it toward me. Shit, we're all dead, I thought— the whole fuckin' jungle's goin' up in—

CHAPTER FOURTEEN

Eight hours later, on the other side of the world, a cab rolled to a stop on a sleepy tree-lined avenue in a little Oklahoma town.

A captain in an immaculate dress uniform got out of the cab. He was holding the telegram by the córner because his hands were all sweaty.

Why do they have to use a captain to deliver the bad news, he thought; why not a lieutenant or even an NCO? He had to ride herd over a whole company of clerks at Fort Sill, on top of delivering these telegrams. It wasn't fair.

He checked the number on the house and compared it with the one on the telegram. Mrs. Beatrice Farmer, 2705 Central Avenue.

At least it was a son this time, not a husband. Widows are harder to calm down.

He started up the walk and told himself that he had the hardest job in the world.

VIETNAM

NOVELS WRITTEN BY
MEN WHO WERE THERE

THE BIG V William Pelfrey   67074-7/$2.95
"An excellent novel...Mr. Pelfrey, who spent a year as an infantryman in Vietnam, recreates that experience with an intimacy that makes the difference."
The New York Times Book Review

WAR GAMES James Park Sloan   67835-7/$2.95
Amidst the fierce madness in Vietnam, a young man searches for the inspiration to write the "definitive war novel." "May become the new *Catch 22*." *Library Journal*

AMERICAN BOYS Steven Phillip Smith   67934-5/$3.50
Four boys come to Vietnam for separate reasons, but each must come to terms with what men are and what it takes to face dying. "The best novel I've come across on the war in Vietnam."
Norman Mailer

BARKING DEER Jonathan Rubin   68437-3/$3.50
A team of twelve men is sent to a Montagnard village in the central highlands where the innocent tribesmen become victims of their would-be defenders. "Powerful." *The New York Times Book Review*

COOKS AND BAKERS Robert A. Anderson   87429-6/$2.95
A young marine lieutenant arrives just when the Vietnam War is at its height and becomes caught up in the personal struggle between the courage needed for killing and the shame of killing. An Avon Original. "A tough-minded unblinking report from hell." *Penthouse*

A FEW GOOD MEN Tom Suddick   87270-6/$2.95
Seven marines in a reconnaissance unit tell their individual stories in a novel that strips away the illusions of heroism in a savage and insane war. An Avon Original. "The brutal power of defined anger." *Publishers Weekly*

AVON Paperbacks